NOT SORRY

Sarah Salway is a poet, novelist and journalist based in Kent. A former Canterbury Laureate and RLF Fellow at the LSE, she is the author of three novels, including *Something Beginning With* (Bloomsbury), one collection of short stories and two poetry collections. She is currently a mentor for the Royal Literary Fund and teaches creative writing in the community.

Not Sorry

SARAH SALWAY

Valley Press

First published in 2021 by Valley Press
Woodend, The Crescent, Scarborough, YO11 2PW
www.valleypressuk.com

ISBN 978-1-912436-66-8
Cat. no. VP0187

A CIP record for this book is available from the British Library.

Cover and text design by Peter Barnfather.
Edited by Jo Haywood.

Printed and bound in the UK by TJ Books Limited.

Contents

START

Instructions for reading this story 11

HUNGER

The beautiful view 17

Lily 20

Dictionary of a marriage at war 21

Spider plant questionnaire 23

Pink 25

On hold 27

Why my husband still keeps our dead dog's
    collar in his desk drawer 29

CONTROL

Knitting 33

How to keep the wolf from your mind 35

And in the wild no one can hear you scream 36

Be careful 38

The heart of a siren 42

Not sorry 45

Trees we like 46

Ten ways to build a fire 49

Trunk 51

I will love you forever 54

Monday's child 55

Lost librarians and the whale 57

How he likes me to dress 61

JOURNEY

Rosehip goes on vacation   67
Edward takes his picnic on the bus   68
In the stars   72
Fine   75
The somnambulist   77
Tube   79
The dying art of small wants   80
I come from kitchen tables   83
Safekeeping   84
Catching a train with Godot   86
Waves   88

LOSS

Home   95
The butcher, the tailor's girl and the witch ball   96
Spinning the kaleidoscope   98
Clapping   100
New life   102
Ward back bird black   105
Things that used to feel safe   110
The new Fairbourne paint chart   112
Not every silence needs to be broken   114
George's house has two chimneys   116

HOME

Swoop   121
Buried   123
Go Jack, go   126
Five woodland walks   129
Homegrown   133
Bookmarked   136
Foresight   138
Bull in a china shop   139
Living room   142
All spoke for   143

FINISH

Self-portrait with chocolate   153

Acknowledgements   155

START

Instructions for reading this story

1. Do not assume that just because the story ends with the man and the woman *not* living happily ever after that the author has problems in her own relationship.

2. A cat can sometimes be just a cat. It is not necessarily a metaphor for death, or motherhood, or even Derrida's theory of différance. Perhaps a cat was sitting on the author's desk and the author thought it would be nice to put it in the story because the cat was old and may not be alive when the story was published. On second thoughts, sometimes a cat can be a metaphor for death. But do not make the mistake of assuming you are clever.

3. Likewise the spelling mistake in line seven of the third paragraph on page two may just be a typo that bypassed the author, editor and copy-editor. It is kinder to ignore it rather than suggest students include it in their essays as deliberate faux-beginnerism. And especially not as an example of sloppy editing. In fact, don't teach this story at all. But if you do, do not send the author your students' comments. Unless, of course, they are very positive. And then send them straight away.

4. Please look at the name of the author carefully. Remember it. This person has spent many hours chained to her desk when she would rather be out walking in the woods just so you could be entertained. So if you ever

meet her, don't ask if she has published anything. This may be upsetting for her, especially if it has been a long time and she has just been dropped by her publishing house. But if you forget, don't go on to request the name she writes under. It will be her own. You just won't have remembered it.

5. But if, by some miracle, you do remember the author's name and you also remember she wrote this story, do not talk about that lovely cat – the so-called death metaphor, and how clever it must have been to be able to turn on the kitchen tap and drink from it. Or how sweet it was when it would lie on the second from bottom step just so it could catch the comings and goings of the household. She may still be feeling raw about its death.

6. OK, it probably is safe to assume that when the husband in the story is pushed in front of the oncoming car and the wife just stands by and laughs, that may be a small clue that the author's marriage has not been a success. However, do not assume that the author is a man-hater (see point 9).

7. Or that the fictional husband had a rough deal. He really did not. You remember that paragraph about how he'd smell his food before he ate it, and also the one when he comments in public about the size of his wife's thighs. Think whether you could get that level of detail in prose without there being some element of truth.

8. When the woman throws herself on the bathroom floor and weeps, feel free to notice for a moment the carefully chosen colours of the expensive Italian tiles, the smell of the English lavender soap she inhales, and how clean that floor must have been for her to feel comfortable about lying there for so long. And then cry with her. Do not smile, or wish you could slap her face and tell her how the middle classes have no problems really, or skip to the next paragraph to see how the husband is doing in hospital.

9. That moment when the hot young Italian waiter tells the woman she is too beautiful to weep for a dead husband does NOT come too soon after the husband's eventual demise. In fact, if anything, it has been years in the planning, involving many, many nights of imagining.

10. The woman in this story does not necessarily have a problem with control. Nor is she a hard-hearted money-pinching bitch. She may just find it hard to express her feelings. She is relying on readers to pick up her sensitivity through the old creative writing adage – show, don't tell. Look how much she does for her husband; even arranging a sudden death for him. Remember the cat. On second thoughts, do not mention the cat.

HUNGER

he felt something stirring inside
that he recognised as life

The beautiful view

Once there was and was not a Lord who owned a garden as green as spring and a lake so picturesque that swans flocked to use it as a mirror, with hills tumbling over each other like gentle puppies, and every tree a stroke of God's pencil.

But so much beauty can dull the spirits, and when you are a Lord you do not expect, or indeed know how, to entertain yourself. This Lord thought there was only so much time you could spend looking out at a perfectly formed view or riding through a landscape so deliciously ordered in every way. His Lady disagreed but she too was so beautiful and perfectly formed that the Lord had stopped listening to her long ago.

He complained instead to his mistress, who stroked the wart on her lopsided chin and thought. And as she thought, the Lord looked out of the window of her hobbledygobbledy cottage at a nearby chimney belching smoke towards two unattractive teenagers hanging round a water pump, as teenagers will always do, and he felt the stirrings of something he recognised as life. Visiting his mistress always did this to him.

'I have an idea,' she said.

When he was back at the castle, he ordered his landscape gardener to him. 'This here,' he waved an arm at the well-proportioned park, 'will have to go.'

The Lady gasped, and his landscape gardener pleaded, but the Lord was firm. He even enjoyed this slight disturbance. He'd got so used to everything being organised entirely for his pleasure that he rarely had to do anything anymore but sign the odd cheque.

This time round the Lord did not take his Lady on a Grand Tour but watched as the works were completed. He even had the rooms of his house rearranged so he could stare out at the construction, and destruction, he had ordered.

The villagers came to see him in the same numbers as they had when he originally had the village moved. 'We have grown to love our new place,' they pleaded in vain, 'and our wives all prefer the hobbledygobbledy houses you built us. None of us want to move back.'

He remained firm, and even smiled the first time he heard them swearing in earshot of his bedroom. However, by the time a month was up, the Lord would have given anything for it all to be as it had been. He stared at the chimney belching smoke far too near the drawing room for his liking, and he strode angrily to his mistress's house.

'This was all your idea,' he yelled, flinging open the door. 'I should never have listened to you.'

To his dismay, it was not his mistress before him but his wife and his landscape gardener. As he saw the disarray of her clothing and the shocked expression on his Lady's face, he felt something stirring inside that he recognised as life.

It was, of course, too late.

The Lady had put up with so much from the Lord, and not just recently, that the thought of social isolation with the landscape gardener was a relief.

And the Lord's mistress?

She sent him a sketch from Italy. It was a picture of David, and even two dimensionally, the statue's marble beauty soothed the Lord. No one else knew him as well as his mistress did.

He put it in pride of place on his mantelpiece, adjusting it millimetres this way and that so it was perfectly centred, before doing something he hadn't done for a long, long time. The Lord laughed. And then, before he finally sat down to wait for his mistress to come back, he went to the window to stare at the two unattractive teenagers who were loitering, as teenagers will always do, by the water pump.

Lily

Outside the kitchen window, the day lily grows with every cup of tea you make, exploding from the top of its delicate stalk, cells popping into the early summer air, as loud as the helicopter flying low overhead as later, as you post your library books back one by one, as the sound of each one hits the metal floor of the overnight container, and as the blind man turns to you, asks if you've ever been to Thailand, as he's never had a woman friend before, and arm in arm, you cross the road to his bus stop, as he says he listened to a scary story last night and had to sleep with his hands covering his ears so no more words could post themselves back into his head. It's funny that, he says, not smiling, as he asks if he can cup your chin, as he holds it close to his face as if you're the day lily and he can hear you growing.

Dictionary of a marriage at war

She finds the letters wrapped in a frayed black ribbon that must have come from a box of treats she can't remember. Chocolate maybe. Or perfume. Or lingerie. Not for her anyway. He gave her a food mixer last Christmas, and she was pleased. So she should have been. She'd bought it herself. It was a joke they'd shared for years. How she would pretend to be surprised when she opened her gift. *You basket case*, she reads now. She puts the letter down and picks up another. *I'm spike-bozzled by you.* Is this English? It's his handwriting. Another. *I'm your booby trap.* There are more. *You've hit me with a daisy cutter.* She goes to the computer but stops herself turning it on. Instead she places the letters on the floor and walks round them. There are fifteen. She tries to put them in order, but these words she can't understand won't let her. They are barbed wire on a battlefield. Missiles from an enemy. She writes them down… *Dekko, Dingbat, Crump Hole.* There's something dangerous about them, something furtive. She leaves them in the house when she goes to the post office, buys a packet of envelopes, postage stamps and a new notebook. The first letter she sends back to herself contains the word *Archie*. She opens it in front of him at breakfast, watching him carefully. He does not react. She starts writing her dictionary. *Archie = A man with no courage and soon no wife.* She will leave the notebook out for him when she has sent and received all the letters. B comes tomorrow. *Bond = a vow that's lost its meaning.* The alphabet will tell her side of the story, and his original letters will be lost forever. All she'll leave him is the pulp at the bottom of the food mixer. She imagines his surprise. *Joke = this one's on him.*

Spider plant questionnaire

How old are you?
What is your species designation?
Where are you from?
Have you always been lurking in that corner?
Can you even remember how you got there?
Did someone bring you here against your will?
Or did you creep in through the window like you're
    trying to creep out now?
What is the secret of your survival?
Do you really need so little in life?
And yet what is this need to procreate?
Why do you think that the world needs more of you?
Did you know I looked you up?
Can you even pronounce your official name of
    Chlorophytum comosum?
Which of your common names – airplane plant, St
    Bernard's lily, spider ivy, ribbon plant, and hen
    and chickens – do you prefer?
But whatever you're called, have you no compassion?

Why are you taking over my house?
Do you worry that I have no compassion?
Are you concerned at how easily I could kill you?
Should I lose sleep at how I would feel no shame?
Can you even think, feel?
Can I?
Or perhaps you have too much compassion?

Does it leak from your fleshy crown like all those
    mini spider plants?
Is it true that plants can talk to each other?
Have you tried to support those other plants dying
    around you?
Do you even notice them?
Or are you the ultimate example of selfishness,
    pushing out these babies while taking no responsibility?
Is this what I can learn from you?
What is the name you whisper to yourself at night?
Do you hear me whisper too?

Pink

I want you naked, he said. As if your clothes were just an inconvenience. As if they meant nothing.

So you took them off. Of course you did. This was him. Although you didn't like the way he brushed your skin with the palm of his hand. As if it meant nothing.

And then he left you sitting there. Adjusting the easel, putting out his brushes. As if he couldn't have done any of that before. And all the time there you were. Naked. As if your body meant nothing.

You are not my husband, you told him eventually. He replied that he knew this. Even laughed as if you'd said something amusing.

He is the only person who has seen me like this, you told him.

It was only when he smiled that you noticed how sharp his teeth were.

But soon, he said, *the world will see your body. Maybe you'll be in a gallery, or a grand drawing room, and people will walk by, see you naked and walk on.*

You hoped he would not see you tremble.

Or maybe a bedroom, he said. *You'll hang on their wall and they'll put on their own clothes standing right next to you. Perhaps they won't even notice you after a while. There's nothing to worry about.*

You shut your eyes, your hand resting on your naked thigh. You'd lied. Not even your husband had seen you exactly like this. So much of you. All of you. Meanwhile,

the artist bustled, concentrating on getting the right shade
of pink for your body.

    Look at me, you say, as if he meant nothing.

On hold

She was just passing the phone box the first time it rang.

Or that's what she said afterwards. She checked her mobile of course, but her boyfriend had recently changed her ringtone to 'Barbie Girl'. This was an old fashioned *dring dring*. It brought back so many memories that when she picked up the receiver she almost expected it to be her mother telling her to be careful.

'Hello,' she breathed, 'hello, hello, hello.'

She gently touched the four corners of one of the post-cards plastered on the wall as she waited for the torrent of words in a language she couldn't understand to finish. And then she replaced the receiver.

The second time it rang, she'd been waiting for half an hour.

The phone box wasn't even near her house, but she changed the route of her run so she could pass it. Every third run, she'd wait. Just in case. Her boyfriend complained that she wasn't losing that much weight for someone who ran so much, but she told him it was muscle now.

When the phone rang she didn't say anything at first, just let the voice on the other end run on, smiling at the way it rose and fell, how the consonants tripped over each other. As she listened, she let her fingers trace the women on the postcards. They all looked so happy.

'Sweet dreams, be safe,' she whispered as she replaced the receiver. It was what her mother always used to say to her before she went to sleep.

She threw the cards into the bin by the park. 'Sweet dreams,' she whispered as she imagined them nestling together in the dark.

It was some time before she could go near the phone box again. Her boyfriend insisted on running with her and he liked easier routes, ones he could track on his computer. He liked to run for twenty-five minutes exactly and then have sex for another twenty-five minutes. Ten minutes for a shower. He called it their productive hour. 'I don't understand why you used to take so long,' he kept saying.

It was a relief to run without him. The roads seemed familiar, as if they were welcoming her home, and the phone box gleamed like a red present waiting for her to open it.

There were new girls pasted up, all still smiling though. She was counting them, cataloguing them in her head – brown-haired, Asian, blondes – when the phone rang. *Dring dring.* It came as such a shock that she almost dropped her stack of girls.

It was a different man on the other end this time, but the words were the same. Unintelligible, and such a hard rhythm to the language that she shut her eyes as if that might stop her hearing.

'Sweet dreams,' she whispered. 'Be safe, be safe, be safe.'

She was still talking when the phone box door swung open, an arm grabbing at her, swiping the cards so they fell, forming a circle around her.

Why my husband still keeps our dead dog's collar in his desk drawer

Because someone once told us that having a dog provides an element of necessary chaos

Because the vet handed it to him, after, and he took it without thinking

Because we decided to let the surgery deal with her body

Because he recently saw a woman who looked just like her Alsatian, and he felt happy he never wanted to muzzle our dog (or me)

Because he wonders if we'll ever get another dog and if we did, would it wear this collar?

Because he loved her

Because when he sits still for too long working, he sometimes opens the drawer and thinks about going for a walk

Because this collar made us laugh so much when we first put it on her, how decorative it was, how fancy

Because it was expensive

Because even the thought of another dog wearing this collar is a betrayal

Because we've left it too late now

Because we don't need more chaos in our life

CONTROL

you wonder if you should
have followed a pattern

Knitting

You start simple and cast the husband on first. The bags of pink wool in the cupboard are kept under the stairs, and you tremble a little as you needle in the dark curls, pull the small red strands for his nipples.

Later that night you wonder if you should have followed a pattern. His right shoulder is higher than his left, but at least only you know you ran out of wool and his feet are blue. Next time you'll order more pink.

The house takes longer. You keep changing your mind. The vegetable garden becomes green kitchen units. Halfway through the roof, you pause, rest your wrists, order bigger needles. You use crochet for the chimneys. Important to keep stretching yourself. Your husband nods from his chair. A brain next time, you think. You'd do so many things differently.

Because the truth is you aren't happy. You keep trying new things. A mustard coloured dog, a white conservatory, robins for the bird table. You ransack the internet for a rose pattern, stitch yourself the perfect English garden. The extension you did in stocking stitch gives you somewhere to secrete your new lover. You order more pink wool, just in case.

It doesn't make a jot of difference.

You unpick the husband, amend his shoulders, improve his hand control, increase certain parts, leave the blue feet for sentimental reasons, but still nothing works. That's when you know what you have to do.

The first row is agony. Pain isn't described as piercing needles for nothing. You console yourself that it must get easier as you become softer, so you keep going, drawing the threads of your skin together.

Your fingers are the last bit to do, and just as you're about to give up, the needles clumsily dropping to the floor for the umpteenth time, you feel a nudge at your side, a perfectly aligned upper body reaching forward and taking over.

The roof leaks, there's a strange banging from the extension and you should have stocked up on bird food, but you feel blessed. You are cushioned from life, your head nicely woolly. You've seen your husband rummage in the cupboard under the stairs, watch him stash the rest of the pink wool where he thinks you can't get it. You know he's using your pattern to make himself a new wife, but still you nod at him from your chair, wave at him with your blue fingers.

How to keep the wolf from your mind

First, know what she is. Is her coat shiny and slick, or is she moulting in all the places her jaws find to bite, her hind legs to itch? Does she reach up to howl at the smell of that clementine cake (the one you made just because you miss your children – does your wolf have a family?) cooling on the kitchen table? Don't ask her. Don't make her real. Tell her lies. Promise you'll carry on for more than a paragraph, a page, even if there's a news story breaking with more figures you won't trust, that doesn't make sense. Stick to words, one sentence at a time. See where they take you both. Let her sniff around the seeds you've planted. Does she think you should have chosen more flowers too? Does she know the value of beauty, or is she hoping to tear limb from limb the rabbit you're planting lettuce for? Because who would notice one less rabbit? Don't go there. Think yourself lucky instead that your wolf has shown herself to you so early and in daylight. Don't question if others can see her. She's yours, make friends with her. Your wolf may not know kindness but she knows survival. Share your cake with her. Ask what story she'd like to hear. Whether she can see the dots on the hellebore flower too, the ones sprinkled as if by a wayward paint brush. Don't think about learning to talk wolf, even though you have the time now. Give her rabbit. Don't look away. This is life too. Go there.

And in the wild no one
can hear you scream

Get your coat, you've pulled, he said. Should I tell someone where we're going, she said. Here's my car, he said. Green Audi CFM 157W, she said. Put your seatbelt on, I'm taking you to paradise, he said. Wow, it's miles from anywhere, she said. Soon be home, he said. How lonely those trees look, standing on their own in the middle of the field like that, she said. Never thought about it, he said. Do you live alone, she said. Here we are, he said. Is that a dog barking, she said. Don't worry he's on a chain, he said. I'm not scared, she said. Fancy some tea, he said. I've got no signal, she said. Or there's some wine in the fridge, he said. You've got a nice house, she said. Don't sound so surprised, he said. So, do you do this often, she said. Leave that photo alone, he said. Must be strange being a farmer, she said. Washing my hands like this is just a habit, you'll have to forgive me, he said. Are you crying, she said. That's a picture of my wife, I took it just before she died, he said. It's a long time since a woman's been here, she said. I thought you might help me, he said. You've done alright for yourself though, she said. I told myself just once, a spur of the moment thing, he said. I can always spot them, she said. You were on your own too, that's why I noticed you, he said. That nervous twitch of desperation under a veneer of over-confidence, she said. I could do with another glass myself, he said. So what's the most valuable thing you own,

36

she said. The courage to get up every morning, he said. Nice knives, she said. They were my wife's, he said. Then try to think of this as a blessing, she said. Do you do this often, he said. Get your coat, she said. The police are just a call away, he said. If there was any signal, she said.

Be careful

Pease pudding hot …

You follow the squares of the hand-painted hopscotch boxes in the empty playground, your steps zigging in and out with every white line. The top of a kid's vacuum flask lies abandoned over by the railings, a piece of lined paper screwed up into a ball in front of you, some broken glass by the verge. You resist the urge to pick up, clear away, keep things safe. You walk on. The bones of the corset he told you to wear dig into your skin. Your ribs are squeezed together by laces tied as tight as you can bear. Without thinking, you hum the rhythm of the childhood skipping game you used to play. Perhaps the children sang these words here this afternoon. Before they rushed home to where they were safe.

Pease pudding cold …

You come alive with every note he writes. That's all it takes. A simple email with an address, date and time to meet. Sometimes he gives brief instructions on what to wear. Once, on the bench outside the hospital, Saturday, 11.30pm, in a white laboratory coat, he made you wait for hours. You watched the walking wounded appear one after the other. All those weekend hopes gone wrong. And the way they looked at you in your white coat, as if you were someone who could help, but you had to keep looking past them. Later, when he kissed your tears away, it just made you cry more.

Pease pudding in the pot ...

You told him about your childhood early on. How it was unusual because your parents were kind, hardworking, lenient enough to let you explore life but clever enough to call you back just when you wanted them to. How you studied a subject you loved at university and then went on to a good career. How you had never dared to do anything really bad. Even the book you stole at school made you feel so sick that you put it back on the teacher's desk the next morning before anyone noticed. You told him about the skipping games you played as a kid, the songs you'd made up, the friends you had. Lots of friends. Because you were popular.

Ten days old.

You sit down now with your back resting against the pole of the basketball hoop, arching your spine so you can feel how tightly your body is caged in this costume. Your fingers pick out the tiny pebbles from the asphalt. There are always the odd ones that can be dislodged if you work them hard enough.

Some like it hot ...

You'd like to meet him in normal places. A pub or a restaurant, or even for the two of you to sit through a film together. He took you to a cinema once, but you only made it as far as the car park. You wore pearls, a black shift dress and high-heeled shoes without tights, and he made you kiss a teenage boy he'd found somewhere. The boy was trembling, at least an inch shorter than you, and it was just a kiss, a light one, but afterwards you saw the boy wipe his mouth on his sleeve again and again, the horror on his face when he turned round at the other side of the car park and saw you both still there. Watching him.

Some like it cold ...

He sees into minds. That's what he tells you. He sees people's fantasies. He sees your fantasies, even the ones you don't admit to yourself. Especially those ones. He says he can make them come true for you.

Some like it in the pot ...

He made you wait for weeks before he sent you tonight's instructions. At first, the lack of contact was a relief. You got on with your own life. You stopped checking the inbox every fifteen minutes. You even thought you might join the people at work for Friday drinks. Make new friends. Be normal. Ordinary. *Hello*, that's all his first email said. So you could have ignored it if you'd really wanted to. *Hello*, you wrote back. And then you cancelled the arrangements you'd made, stopped talking to people in the office, avoided the few friends you had left. He didn't like it when he had to share you. Somehow he knew. Even when he wasn't with you, he knew.

Five days old.

And then he asked you to meet him here. The pebble your nails have been digging away at finally comes loose. You trace the mark it leaves, rubbing the hole backwards and forwards with your fingertips. He's told you he'll always be one step ahead of you.

This hurts me more ...

But a playground? Be prepared, he'd told you. Be prepared for anything I throw at you. You remember the look on his face when you'd told him about your happy childhood, how you had always felt safe. And today you can't run away. Not in these shoes. Your skirt is too narrow for a normal stride. All the clothes you are wearing are ones he chose.

Than it hurts you.

What happens next is your choice. You shut your eyes, try to hear the children's voices echoing through the games that have been played here. Try to hear a voice that might once have been you laughing.

What you wish for.

You want to see if he really can read your mind. Whether he really can make all your fantasies come true. You hear his footsteps. You don't turn, just wait for him to come towards you. You're ready now.

The heart of a siren

He sent his wife out to the corner shop on Sunday morning to buy herself a new heart.

You've not been yourself recently, he told her. It'll do us both good to have a new beat in this marriage.

But straight after she'd gone, he realised how cold the kitchen felt before she made breakfast. He was just picking up the phone to ring her when she came back to say they were fresh out of women's hearts, but she'd managed to get him a nice male one. He told her he'd think about putting it on after she made his porridge.

In, she said. You don't put a heart on, you take it in.

He was astonished. Was she talking back to him? But now she was fussing over something in the knife drawer.

You've not put my heart in there, have you? he asked.

She nodded.

You want to take better care of it, he warned, but she couldn't have heard him because she slammed the drawer shut. Still, for all her faults, his wife was good with oatmeal. As he spooned it up, he couldn't stop looking at the drawer. He could have sworn there was a rhythmic jangle of cutlery coming from it, but the strange thing was that it wasn't unpleasant.

And you're sure it's male? he asked.

He had to turn his head to see her nod. He didn't mind that she always stood behind him while he was eating because once he overheard her on the phone to her sister saying she couldn't abide his table manners. He hadn't said anything; it was easier just to get the phone disconnected the next day. As he often liked to say, silence is the secret of a good marriage. In more than one way.

Men have smaller hearts than women, she said then.

There was something in this comment that felt insulting but he couldn't put his finger on it, so he muttered something about having a bigger brain than her. He was distracted by the noises that were very definitely coming from the drawer now. It sounded as if they were speeding up in a way that made him worried about the health of the heart. If he did decide to use it, then he wanted something that was fresh and new. No knackered old organs for him, no sir.

Can you hear that? he asked.

She lifted her head and shut her eyes as if listening, but she just looked annoyed. She'd got into the habit of always finding fault these days.

Hear what? she asked, clearing his bowl. But even above her clatter, he could almost taste the metallic sound of the heart as it banged this way and that amongst the knives. The tingles it sent through his veins felt like it was beating away inside his body already. He had a strange urge to rescue it.

Have you got a stomach ache? his wife asked. You look pained.

He told her he was just thinking, and she snorted. She tried to pretend she was coughing, but he heard her right enough. It was as if his hearing had been turned up to maximum. He could swear he even heard a sliver of ice tumble inside the freezer.

And above it all, Jesus, the beat beat beat of the heart. He sent a quick apology up to his mother for the blasphemy, but if he was honest, it was more like a prayer. He gripped the seat of his chair and held on so tight his knuckles went white. The hairs on his arms stood up as if to attention, and he felt another rousing as his body tried to burst out of his pyjamas.

For heaven's sake, cover yourself, said his wife quickly.

Where did you find the heart? he managed to blurt out.

At the back of the shop, she said, in amongst the bottled water. Ahab's been doing a special post-Valentines offer so he was surprised to find there was one left.

She stopped and stared at him as he got up from the table and moved towards the drawer. He didn't seem to have any control over his hands so he was still holding tight to the chair; a ship he pulled across the room with him, swaying from side to side, anchorless. His mouth opened and shut like a fish, but no sound came out. Or if it did, he couldn't hear it. All he could hear was the heart beating. Great ocean rolls of beating.

He'd read that a woman will leak milk for months after a stillborn child. And that an amputee feels the itch in a missing limb years after it's gone. He wasn't sure if this heart was claiming his body or the other way round, but there seemed nothing he could do about it.

Because just then, with a burst of freedom as he finally shook off the chair, he opened the drawer. He had just enough time to look back over his shoulder at his wife who was still standing behind him, watching, smiling, before he felt his body rip open to let the heart slip in. For a long, beautiful second, he was complete, finally, before the crescendo of a wave crashed over him.

Not sorry

He is so much smaller than her that she gets embarrassed, wondering if from behind he looks like her child, a hunched up boy in adult clothes like some kind of war refugee, and if so, when he kisses her, do strangers gasp, hurry past so they can see her from the front, and he does kiss her often because it makes him smile to stand on tiptoes, to reach up and take her by the shoulders that are so much wider than his own, and though in anyone else, her reluctance to meet his lips would be cruel, it seems to make him more determined, although she's never told him about the child thing, or how once, when she saw their reflection in the glass, he looked like a little wizened monkey climbing up her great stout oak of a tree, and how she would have pushed him off straight away but he stopped kissing her suddenly, bent down to wipe the dust off the tips of his black leather shoes, such small shoes, and she'd stood still, still looking at the reflection, just her now, alone, the moon making a perfect halo round her head and her lips tingling so much that, in the window, she saw her hand come up and touch them, her tingling lips, her fingertips smoothing her mouth like a salve, searching in vain for the one spot, any spot, he'd missed.

Trees we like

(NB: The words in italics are adapted from an article in Psychology Today, *12 Ways to Find Out If You're the Kind of Person Others Like*, April 2019)

The ash sapling leaves are trembling as it picks up the magazine page that's caught on its bark. It isn't smart enough yet to understand what the words mean, but it still feels as if someone has seen deep inside its trunk. It nudges the great oak next to it and blows the paper across. In a deep voice that rumbles through the forest, the oak starts to read:

'Everyone likes trees who make them feel good. When you're around a tree who allows you to feel capable, well-respected, and fun, you automatically feel that you'd like to spend more time in that forest. On the other hand, when you're with trees who constantly criticise you and point out your weaknesses, you'll try to stay away from them.'

The two willows by the river start to weep. 'Do shut up,' shouts the lone sycamore, until with a sigh, the oak continues:

'Perhaps you know a tree who you see from time to time at arboreal celebrations and each time you begin what you think should be a pleasant conversation, she shoots you down almost immediately.'

The sycamore lets loose a hail of helicopter seeds, and the oak nods. Perhaps he'd been a bit pointed. In a softer growl, he reads on:

'What is it about trees who are so demeaning that every inter-action results in you feeling bad about yourself? Trees who are strong on the quality of encouragement can express positive messages to others, usually through language, to help another tree address a challenging situation or realise their potential.'

The ash can see that the oak is pretending not to notice the smallest stickiest lime edging closer. At least the predicted storm will help clear even the most tenacious residues.

'Flipping now to the way you're perceived by others, can you honestly determine whether you've managed to win trees over with your own positive messages?'

The trees bend in, their top branches gently touching so a passing squirrel misses its footing and falls. Underground, their roots are trembling, good feelings passing from one tree to another. This is better than the last article they'd found which had been called *Carving in bark.*

'By being encouraging to other trees, you stand to benefit as well. Getting trees to like you is certainly one of those benefits, because it sets in motion its own cycle of positivity.'

And just at that moment, a gust of wind blows the paper out of the oak's branches and towards the hawthorn hedge. The willows stop weeping for a minute, and the sycamore halts its shaking. They all watch as the shrubbiest hawthorn of them all puts out a root and catches the paper. Nothing good will come from this; the hawthorn has been taking its border patrol duties seriously since it finished flowering. It slowly and elaborately smells the now crumpled sheet. 'It's made from pine,' she says. 'And not even from around here. Back as you were.' The trees are silent, their crowns a circle of patient, if hopeless, positivity, reaching up together as the first drops of rain start to fall.

Ten ways to build a fire

The inside history of the Instacinders brand

1. ALLOW SERENDIPITY. The thing with the shoe got them so many likes and it wasn't even planned. That's how it all started really.

2. LEARN FROM MISTAKES. When sponsors started calling and Cinders' phone was out of juice, Buttons became the middle man. Actually her post about that was perhaps where it really started. *Always keep your phone charged, girls!* Not the wittiest Insta comment admittedly but by then anything Cinders posted became a sensation.

3. THINK AHEAD. The first major deal was with a magazine, and included rights for the wedding. Cinders could have told them that there wasn't a hope in hell of the Palace agreeing but before she could get involved, another problem raised its head.

4. TAKE CARE OF THE PAPERWORK. It turned out she'd signed some kind of publicity contract with the God-mother. 'I thought it was just for the travel stuff,' Cinders pleaded, but it was pretty all-encompassing – food, clothes, hair, makeup. 'We're ruined,' Buttons moaned.

5. GET TO KNOW YOUR AUDIENCE. Cinders and Buttons took a selfie by the fireplace covered only in ashes. The symbolism went way over the heads of her target audience. Only 7,000 likes, and as many negative comments about too much dirt.

6. REMEMBER TO BREATHE. To help Cinders, Stepmother threatened to call in the lawyers but Godmother remained firm. She'd taken up yoga since the pumpkin incident and was infuriatingly calm.

7. FOSTER SELF-RESPONSIBILITY. Meanwhile, the Prince was hopeless. He spent more time talking to his vegetables than he did on his social media platform. Cinders had to take care of everything.

8. BE PREPARED... Buttons arranged an exclusive with the magazine to calm everything down. He and Cinders practiced for hours, talking about how Godmother was overly controlling and only out for what she could get.

9. ...FOR ANYTHING. But before that could happen, the mice claimed they'd been bullied into cross-species dressing and different lawyers got involved.

10. YOU ARE IN IT FOR THE LONG HAUL. And then it turned out the Prince had booked an internet-free honeymoon. 'Just you and me,' he purred in that lo-fi way he had, 'happy ever after.' She wanted to be sick but Buttons told her she still had a public to please. Besides there was a wedding exclusive to plan. 'What do you think about a honeymoon baby? Babies are very in at the moment,' Buttons suggested. 'A fresh ending,' she agreed.

Trunk

The new lover I got from the internet came pre-programmed to surprise me, but being jumped out at from behind doors wasn't quite what I had in mind so I sent him back for adjustments.

'Do you want him to cook?' the guy on the help desk asked in a broad Scottish accent. He sounded bored but it was important that I got this right. I'd saved up for months for the top quality model.

'I'm a cordon bleu cook,' I said. 'I live in a home I've designed from scratch, and I earn a six figure salary. I don't want to boast but I am also an expert masturbator, so it's the extras I am looking for.'

I heard the gasp when I mentioned masturbation so I guessed he was one of the human ones that hadn't made the cut to move out of the factories. This interested me. I'd never actually talked to a Loser in real life.

'What might those be?' he asked. I was right. He sounded more interested than before.

'I would like to come home and find presents,' I said, shutting my eyes so I could imagine it better. 'Not just flowers or chocolates, but something I've never seen before. Perhaps even something I didn't know I wanted.'

'Presents,' he said, as if he was writing it down.

'And I would like him to have opinions,' I said. 'Not stupid ones, but ones that make me change my own mind.'

'Opinions,' he repeated.

I was getting into my stride. 'And he needs to make me laugh,' I said.

'Laughter?' he queried. 'You're probably asking a little too much here if it's the male model you want.'

To my surprise, I laughed.

The metal trunk sat on the doorstep the following week. No paperwork, but the label had my name on it.

I tried to open the lid. No luck.

There was something inside; I heard the shift of something heavy as I dragged it into the house. It must be my adjusted new lover, but this wasn't the best start. Less of a surprise than an annoyance. I kicked it, and heard a yelp from inside.

'Are you OK?' I asked, but when there was no reply, I went to pour myself a glass of wine. What with one thing and another, it was only when I was in bed later that I remembered the trunk.

Oh well, I'd open it in the morning. It was only when I officially turned my lover on that he would come properly to life. One night wouldn't hurt anyone.

I was woken the next morning by the doorbell. When I opened the door, there was my new lover. He held a book out to me.

'Rumi,' I said, nicely surprised.

'I know them all,' he whispered. 'Just tell me what page and I will whisper the words in your ears.'

What with one thing and another, it was two days before I remembered the trunk again.

'What do you think it is?' I asked my now not so new lover.

'Shall I open it for you?' he asked, pulling out an enormous toolbox. There's always something special about a man with his own toolbox so we went back to bed, and it was four hours later that we tackled the trunk together.

'Am I a nice surprise?' my lover asked as he prised open the lid. He had a wrench in one hand and was flexing the muscles of his other arm.

My nodding was curtailed however when I saw the body lying in the bottom of the trunk. It was wearing a kilt, and held a bunch of wilted flowers in one hand.

'I think it might be Phil, the guy from the help desk,' I said.

'He's not going to be much help to anyone anymore,' my lover said. 'Shall we get rid of it?'

'It?' I don't know why this word upset me so much. 'Phil's human.'

'A dead Phil,' my lover said, holding out his arms as if he was going to scoop me up. 'But don't cry. Let me make you feel better.'

'How can you think about sex now?' I shouted. 'There's a dead man in my hall.'

'And a live one ready to take you to bed,' my lover cooed.

'You're not a man,' I said. 'You're a lover.'

But before I could say any more, my lover lifted me up and threw me over his shoulder. It seemed his muscles were not just for show, and he'd been well programmed. As he took me through to the bedroom, he started to tell me what he thought about climate change. The figures he was quoting made my head swim, and despite myself, I began to listen.

We're reasonably happy, my lover and I. If I could forget about the help desk guy folding himself into the trunk and posting himself to me, I'd be ecstatic. To tell the truth, the stupidity of that gesture never fails to make me laugh, but I guess you can't have everything.

I will love you forever
(an acrostic)

Ian's leaving the office. Work has become his sanctuary recently, the only place he can get away from things. Incoming calls that block his phone. Lingerie left draped on the door of his flat. Lawyers' letters so badly faked he wants to laugh. 'Let her get bored of it,' his friends advise when he gets to the pub. Other people have, it seems, similar stories of lovers who won't take no for an answer. Vengeance is a dish best served cold, one of his mates says after their second bottle of wine. Even hellish women get angry, another friend corrects, and both burst out laughing as they fall off their chairs. You're best rid of her, they say, and he wants to cry that he's not rid of her, that's the problem. Only leaving the country seems an option. Uncaring, she called him. Forensic in his dumping of her. Or not-dumping, because she won't go. Revenge, his friend is saying now, I'm sure there's something about revenge and women and hell. Every man should have it carved on their forehead, his other friend says. Visible as a reminder of the consequences of mixing with the wrong kind. Except, if he's being honest, she wasn't the wrong kind, not at first; she was smart, beautiful and he couldn't believe that someone like her would even look at someone like him. Remember me, he hears a voice behind him, looks round, sees who it is, screams.

Monday's child

The robot that came on Monday was a disgrace...
It had been programmed for joy and leisure, flirted with my husband and refused to do the laundry. Eventually, after it insisted on using our staircase for pole dancing practice, I keyed in the return address and sent it away.

Tuesday's smelt of mace...
What with Monday's robot returning twice in the night, and the company refusing to take any responsibility. Robot 2, which had arrived – to its initial credit – in apologetic mode, was annoying the hell out of me by lunchtime, always cringing in the corner, and besides, where was my husband?

Wednesday's was like watching Psycho...
The minute I got into the shower, I found Monday's robot already there before me. 'Turn round,' it squeaked, its hands feeling my body, 'this helps to see what he once liked.' I screamed. Robot 2 hid before I could call the police, but Monday's robot merely slipped away, taking my sandalwood soap with it.

Thursday's still a shadow...
Of course, the company's lawyers said they had no control over rogue robots, and because I had kept Robot 2 for more than two days, I couldn't return it for a braver model. And then the police said apparently missing husbands were becoming increasingly common. 'Men,' the desk officer told me,

55

'prefer easier lives these days, ones without all that emotion.' I thought of Monday's robot's hands in the shower, the give of the soft rubber exterior, the strength beneath, and I shuddered.

Friday was all heads shaking, hands wringing…
I cried all day, sitting in my armchair, Robot 2 kneeling at my feet with sweet tea and tissues.

Until Saturday came out swinging…
Robot 2 came up simpering with a postcard signed by Monday's robot from Margate. *Having lovely time. Your husband now mine.* I couldn't believe how Robot 2 just stood there. 'Are all you machines programmed for competition,' I asked it, 'or is she an aberration?' Robot 2 fluttered its eyelashes. 'We have been trained to pick up a human's basest needs,' it whispered, 'what it's not getting, and how we can help.' I stared at it. 'What do you think I need?' I asked, but I was scared I already knew.

And so it was Sunday who let the robots stay,
and even for a moment, let us play…
My husband came back immediately when I called him with my suggestion. I was pleased to see Monday's robot turned off and lying inert in the back of the car because I would have lost my nerve if it had been perched on the passenger seat. Robot 2 rushed out to open the doors, looking at me the whole time to check I was happy. 'We will keep Monday's robot for weekends,' I told my husband, 'and emergencies.' We held hands in a circle, the four of us, soft hard soft hard. As we let go and turned to walk towards the house, I pretended not to see how the two robots winked at each other behind our backs.

Lost librarians and the whale

> *Lock up your libraries if you like;*
> *but there is no gate, no lock,*
> *no bolt that you can set upon*
> *the freedom of my mind.*
> – Virginia Woolf, *A Room of One's Own*

Canterbury 2025

Hello, and thank you for coming to the twenty-third reunion of the Librarians Reshelving Themselves Society, incorporating the former Dewey Dolls, Bookbag Boys and the Party for the Protection of the Semi-Colon.

Yes, welcome to this meeting where the past is always tense, and the future is perfect. I'm delighted to learn that our security guards only had to restrain two guests at the door for illegal adverbial activity, and also to reassure you that the twenty-six members of the Alphabetised and Proud Librarians have been censured due to the disruption of secondary redundancies in their title.

How different it is from those dark days before 2019 when our beloved department was first formed to enforce semantic rules. No coincidence that it was also the year poets finally realised that no one had noticed they had been on strike since 2018, and we could finally allow the novelists the space they had always claimed to crave and rehome them in the woods that had been steadily regrowing into things of beauty once we no longer needed an endless supply of paper. Of course, for several months afterwards, the short story writers continued to rush between different camps until they exploded with perhaps the first and only truly satisfying flash on record. But no one in this room ever knew where to place them anyway, so I think we can all agree that it was a blessed relief.

You will, I'm sure, have already noticed our first gift to you: the space and beauty offered by this wall of empty shelves. We have taken the liberty of protecting their symbolism with electric shock wires.

And over there on the right-hand side, you see one in use already. Sir, the Tattooed Librarians meet on Fridays when extra guards are available. And no one is listening to you – your pathetic attempt to draw support by leaving ellipses in your rhyming couplets are in vain. The folk in this room are an altogether main clause. All nouns, no action – that's now our slogan, after all, and has been since Library Cuts forced us to lose the second part, that unnecessary rhetorical question – where are the verbs?

But look, our uninvited guest has left an industrialised information packet behind, from where he tried to place it on the shelf. Please bring it to the front. Ah, *Moby Dick*. At least it's something thick with which to start tonight's furnace – one of the many reasons to thank our leader, Periscope Tumbler, because isn't this warmth nicer than feeling the chill of other people's messy, and sometimes grammatically incorrect, words?

I believe Mr Melville has incidences of using who instead of whom on at least every other page, calling it, if you will, voice. There are sentences beginning with an injunction, and even preposition phrases used instead of an adverb modifying the other adverbs. Imagine if our children got hold of a text like this. Just visualise the chaos of future generations of students being educated without a full and comprehensive knowledge of grammar, having to rely instead on the illusion of story.

Or as it was once even defended in the paper age – a simple love of story. A phrase which we now know is as abstract as porridge. So much better to depend on a complicated evaluative algorithm rather than the oxymoron of simple love.

Perhaps all of us in this room were once examples of how such passive thinking gets you – if I may use a deliberately provocative incohesive device – nowhere?

Apologies for the joke. Never let it be said that representatives from the Department of Grammar As a Form Of Imagination Control (or as it's better known, DOG AFOC) have no sense of humour.

But where was I going? Common nouns – was ever a description more accurate? To think we once classified our naming words without pure knowledge of determiners or how past participles could be used both as perfects and passives, optional preposition phrases or indeed contrasts with complements. It makes me shudder when I think how we once believed in the pagan mysteries of rhythm, repetition and rhetoric.

And progress couldn't have happened without you in this room, and how, after the last library closed, you endured a time of status re-education, enforced Twitter boarding and YouTube feeding. A tough sentence maybe, but one that saved our sentences, to use a humorous homophone. Even subordinate words became safe again as the use of intransitive phrases was monitored and stressed in every tense.

And it worked, because look how none of you came forward just now to save the cowardly whale which of course we had placed on the shelf ourselves as a test. We had expected modified restraints, at the very least a subjunctive mood, but you have proved we can now feel confident that a book is just a book, a manufactured menace. The closure of its covers means our word family can breathe again, related through morphology back to our roots and meaning into one just line – constantly evaluated and adapted by the National Curriculum. Thankfully now we can change any text anywhere in the world at any time to something more currently appropriate with just one click.

But enough history. Since the beginning when we first welcomed emoticons into our dictionaries, we are all about moving forward. So let's give a huge *thumbs up* to our sponsors, the only book we need and the 24-7 keeper of our thoughts, dreams and yes, stories – Mindbook!

How he likes me to dress

It's backless, green, thick thick satin.

It's how I've always wanted you to look, he told me in the shop. And I knew it was true. The dress is that bright emerald green film stars wear to contrast with red carpets. Shining. Plunging down just beyond the point of safety at the front. He loved it so much he didn't wait to hear what I thought.

I drape it on the bed and shape it as if I'm dancing inside. One hip swaying slightly to the left as if it's searching for another body, swaying in the way that calls to be stopped, swaying the way I rarely dare any more in real life. At least not when he's watching. He prefers me to stand still so he can look at me. Like an object. Or a possession.

I spread out the hem so it kicks up one heel behind and leave it like that to wait for when he comes back. I'll let the dress simper up to him. *Look at me, I'm so beautiful. See what an effort I've made. Just for you.*

Do I give the dress a backwards look as I leave the bedroom? Not for one second. I imagine it straining to sit up on the other side of the shut door, muscleless despite the heavily boned corset. *Hey,* it'll scream, its voice too shrill just as the green is a little too bright away from the shop's fluorescent lights. *Let's get this party started.*

I stand and stare at myself in the hall mirror before bending down and pulling the laces on my black boots a little tighter.

Heels are nice, the dress shouts from the bedroom. *Your feet hurt like hell but it flatters the calves. And you know he always looks at women's legs.*

I smooth both hands along the front of my legs from my thighs to my ankles, feeling the wool of my thick black tights warm against my fingers.

Sheer stockings, it yells. *And suspenders. He likes to glimpse those thin slivers of flesh.*

A black t-shirt and denim shorts. I feel ready for anything.

He prefers to have something to undo. The dress sounds as if it is breathing heavily now. *Not too obvious. You must always present a man with a challenge. A row of tiny buttons to fumble with or interlocking ribbons.*

I undo the buckle on my belt and slide it out of the waistband. Better.

Remember jewellery, the dress squawks. *Too many women forget that your earrings, necklace and bracelet should match. Neatness is so important to him.*

I rub my bare neck. Pull my bare earlobes.

You'll want your hair up. Show off your neckline. Just leave some tendrils falling down at the back. It takes forever but it's worth it when he feels he only has to touch a strand for it all to collapse.

I run both hands through my newly cropped hair, leaving it standing up around my face like a dandelion. Like a halo. Now in the mirror, I seem to be able to see myself more clearly, more openly, than I have for a long time. Hello, I nod at my reflection. Hello, you.

Perhaps some perfume? Something sophisticated and ladylike he can remember you by.

The dress's voice drops down to a whisper as I take the stairs two by two.

You'll, you'll…

I pause briefly at the front door. It's as if I'm expecting to catch the click of the bedroom door opening and the sound of heavy satin swish-swish-swishing down behind me.

Silence.

Outside I gulp the fresh air down as if I'm starving. And then I run.

JOURNEY

from the status quo, the silent majority,
upturned dishes and broken glass

Rosehip goes on vacation

Essential to wait until the first bloom is over/ for my petals to stop bruising/ falling like dew/ past lengthening shadows/ the butterfly/ feasting on that buddleia all summer/ take take take/ no wonder I've become rigid/ small and stony/ not all transformations are beautiful/ even my perfume dulls/ but I've seen what can happen/ sisters cut down/ I wait for that moment the world turns away/ and that's when I go/ take the hedgerow to the countryside/ the wild path to the sea/ I strip off/ dive into dreams/ that old tale/ thorns lifting like towers in a fairytale castle/ where an ancestor lived/ swapped for a daughter/ kept in a bell jar/ for what?/ not dying exactly/ stepping over into a new story/ sometimes I just need to get out of the garden/ grab a break/ take a breath/ and another/ room to stretch now/ a fertile bomb/ packed hard with seeds/ my own rawness/ (oh, the sky is so blue).

Edward takes his picnic on the bus

He keeps his bag on the seat beside him so he can dip into it every now and then, pull out a silver foil wrapped package and …

… ohhh …

… a hard-boiled egg with …

… yes …

… a twist of salt.

To tell the truth, he's often thought about leaving out the egg after those two women complained about the smell that one time.

'I thought he was farting, Caroline.'

'I didn't like to think.'

They were giggling as if he was the entertainment.

'Oh my god, Caroline,' the loud one went. 'He's got a chicken leg now.'

He-he-he-he-he.

And so that time he didn't gnaw down to the bone as he normally did.

'Caroline, it's a, what is it, can you see?'

He neatly folded the silver paper.

'It's a fucking pineapple, Caroline.'

After the egg comes smoked salmon sandwiches, the thinnest brown bread, a scraping of butter followed by a shake of black pepper. He delves into his bag and squeezes what's left until he's sure he's got the lemon.

These are things someone like Caroline wouldn't know. How much these touches matter. Like the little sprig of dill with the salmon. Just enough to tickle his mouth and surprise him.

No, don't think of Caroline today. Breathe deeply. Then into the bag and …

… cream …

… pastry …

… a layer of raspberry jam …

… sugar.

Sugar me, mille-feuille.

Ahhh.

This isn't a picnic for the faint-hearted. This is a feast. He spends hours every night making sure it's perfect. And in the morning, he closes his eyes to surprise himself, choosing just ten from a possible choice of twenty foil-wrapped packages. He always limits himself to ten. Not eleven. Not nine.

It's taken years to be this self-disciplined.

Now the cake is finished, he pulls out the pineapple.

He doesn't eat it. Who do you think he is? No, it provides the element of drama every meal needs. In Georgian times, hosts would hire pineapples for parties as a centrepiece for the table.

But today he has a different drama in mind.

Because it's now he searches for that mystery package he found in the fridge this morning. He places the pineapple on top of his bag so it almost reaches his shoulder. He can feel the foliage stroke his anorak as he opens the …

ALIVE!

Crawling. White. Bloodless.

It's the lamb chop he had lightly grilled with rosemary months ago.

A grain of rice climbs across to the pineapple before he recovers himself. Scrunching the whole package in his hands so he can capture the maggots, the meat, the foil before throwing it behind him.

He lurches forward, stumbles down the stairs. Someone presses the bell, but the shouting and screaming from the top deck forces the bus to a halt anyway.

He starts to walk home.

He needs to clean his mouth and there's an orange waiting patiently for him in his bag.

In the stars

It was the astrologers who benefited the most when the Government decided to cancel April and May.

Everyone had agreed that something had to be done as a result of the extreme climate emergency. Seasons had been speeding up for years, and besides a shorter spring and summer meant that we had more nights – proportionally – to study stars.

We'd all become mad about stars and signs. Even scientists would do tarot readings before experiments and most of us openly wore our star signs on badges. Obviously the carnivores saw this decree as a conspiracy, getting rid of Taureans meant losing one of the two red meat signs, but they were always angry anyway.

Bob, my own Taurean, treated it with more equilibrium than I did. As a fire starter, I knew Aries folk would always be safe, but it was still a shock to watch him open the official letter with his new date of birth so casually. I was now married to a Libran. It has its advantages, he said, weighing both sides of the argument. I could already tell this was going to be maddening.

In the meantime, the chaos around us reflected how I was feeling.

At the beginning of it all, when teenagers still had enough fight left to say 'we told you so,' most people over 30 trusted Government to know what to do. Or at least we pretended to. We still enjoyed too much the slight frisson we got as we fondled our single-use cups and remembered when

Starbucks sold coffee as well as palm readings and astrological charts. But after the seventh winter of floods, even the Government gave up trying. But what, we muttered, could you expect with a Gemini as leader. The new ten month year was a surprise initiative though, the last gasp of a stuttering candle before it's dark forever more. Maybe it wouldn't have mattered as much earlier but, as we struggled for survival, our birth signs became our tribes.

Those foolhardy enough to want to bring children into this world – mostly Scorpions – would ensure they conceived to achieve particular favourable signs for a family unit. Bob and I had only got together after a month of astrological consultations. It had snowed on the August day we married, a favourable sign we'd been told, especially for earth and fire signs. But now that had been changed forever. I was finding out that Librans hated anything they can't control, and besides snow and air do not get on.

Because of the demand, we had to wait three weeks before we could see Stella Stargazer to find out how all this might change the dynamic of our marriage. Around us, couples we knew – even the happiest – were splitting up. Who knew so many placid Taureans felt they'd been in the wrong skin for so long. Even those, like me, who came from more superior signs, were starting to feel like we'd been missing out too. Our gurus, those mostly white men who spoke softly and at length on all channels every night, started shouting that only they, their faces getting increasingly redder and redder, could tell us our destiny. Hadn't we all proved we were incapable of rational decision making?

It was Bob who pointed out that one of the chief gurus had previously been a Taurean like him, but was now a Gemini. And look at that track record, he said with all the self-importance of a new Libran.

I missed my cosy old bull so much, but I had to concede he had a point. And at least he wasn't a Scorpion. They had started to abandon their children on the streets. Bringing up Virgoans wasn't what they had signed up for, it seemed.

By the time our appointment with Stella Stargazer had come round, we were not the only ones to have lost faith in destiny. The syndicated horoscopes we had once rushed to read every morning were left defaced on street corners by artist activists (mostly Aquarians), and the windows of Starbucks were painted with hieroglyphics of bulls.

It wasn't that we didn't still believe, but more that we were refusing to have our identities controlled. This was when the Government played its cleverest move yet. They announced that, before the next election, we had to fill in new census forms. All of us were allowed to choose one of the existing eleven star signs for ourselves, the one we felt fitted us best. Astrologers fumed, but the fluidity appealed to the rest of us.

We became both empowered and inflamed. Self-appointed leaders of each sign held debates enticing us to join them. The voiceless ones (mostly Sagittarians) at last felt listened to. There were so many marches and banners and fights that we were glued to the news every night.

Meanwhile the rain kept falling and all around us the nights were getting longer and longer, but we were far too busy to notice even when the stars stopped shining.

Fine

Before I went on holiday, I locked my emotions in the spare bedroom. It didn't go as easily as I'd hoped. On my way out, I heard Anger shouting at Fear so I kept the taxi waiting while I went back. Lust and Joy were already entwined on the bed while Judgement took notes, so I decided to split them all up. Soon every room in the house was filled and all the doors locked. Getting the right partners together had been exhausting.

'Clock's ticking,' the taxi driver commented when I eventually crawled back to the cab. I looked out of the window to avoid further conversation. Besides, I was busy thinking. Would Doubt and Sadness survive together, and had I been right to put Anticipation and Disgust in the kitchen with all those knives? It could all go horribly wrong but I was amazed that I felt nothing.

'Bet you're excited,' the driver said as we drove into the airport. 'Greece will be lovely right now.' I carried on looking out of the window. I felt no Shame that I was ignoring him, no Satisfaction that … shit, where had I put Satisfaction? Ah well, I let it all slide.

The beach was as it was in the photograph, the sun was shining adequately, the hotel staff seemed keen to make my visit a lovely one. That's what they kept saying. Lovely. Lovely. I repeated it to myself sometimes, but it wasn't as reassuring as I'd hoped.

Only on the last day did I open the box I had locked in my suitcase. Because I'd been panicking, I'd made a last minute decision to bring Romance and Horror with me. None of the other emotions had wanted to be stuck with them and I couldn't blame them. The two were curled foetus-like in the box. I tried to pull Romance out separately – surely it was safe now – but it had fused with Horror so I had to break the box to get them both out. I laid them out, limbs still tangled, on the rush matting and stared. They were desiccated, their skin not just paper thin but actually shredding. They must have sucked each other dry over the five days we'd been on holiday. I tried to worry about this but couldn't. Ah, of course, Worry had stuck to Empathy like a limpet so I'd left them behind, crammed in the bathroom.

I wasn't even surprised. That little minx, Surprise, had sidled up to Nostalgia saying they were both going to have a good kip while I was away.

'Lovely,' I said, going out to the adequate sun and the expected beach for my last walk. I ignored the hotel staff asking what they could do to make my stay memorable. It was all just fine.

The somnambulist

She wakes up to find him holding her feet again. His thumb is rubbing the nail on her big toe, round and round like the sun. He's not looking at her though, his head is stretched back so if she leant forward she could slit his throat. It's a sacrifice, an invitation. If she went to sleep with a knife under her pillow, if she was that kind of woman, she would slit it.

The early morning light is coming through the curtains and the bald patch on his head is shining. She wonders if he even knows it exists. From the front, in the mirror, his hairline must look normal. Shining like the moon, she wants to think; she wants it to be endearing but instead words spill out between them.

'What the fuck do you keep doing with my feet?' she asks, but he's gone back to sleep.

She knows there is such a thing as somnambulism, which doesn't just involve sleepwalking. On one website, she finds the story of a man who drove from Devon to Wales, only to wake up on the ring road round Cardiff. The important thing, she reads, is that you are not to wake the sleeper. It's not safe.

The knife is a kind of joke. She tells herself this. How they will laugh about it together when this 'bad patch' is over.

She tilts her head forward. It's a comfort though, the knife. While she listens to him snore, she tiptoes her fingers under her pillow and tests the blade's sharpness against her skin. The pain eases her. When she wakes up, he has gone, her feet left both cold and unmolested.

At breakfast, she stirs the sugar round and round so her coffee becomes a whirlpool, her cup the world. If she doesn't look up, if she keeps stirring, then everyone will be safe. She imagines him driving round that ring road, round and round. His bald patch shining in the street lights. She presses the blade of her knife against the palm of her free hand, but it's blunt and slippery from the butter she's just spread on her toast. In the mirror behind her, she could swear she looks normal.

Under the table her feet shuffle together as if they wanted to run away, together and apart. Together and…

Tube

They watched. That's what the media will fix on later, but for now there was nothing else they could think of doing. The man had the woman in a headlock, his other hand pulling her hair back so tightly her expression looked blank. Maybe if she'd screamed or fixed on one of them to plead for help, they would have stepped forward, but she didn't, and as the tube doors opened and the man pulled the woman out onto the platform, they watched him drag her down to the exit. Afterwards, one of them – a tourist from Austria – will say he thought this must happen often. A local custom, the journalist will ask so incredulously that the tourist will be forced to lie and say of course not. He won't be able to say what happened next, about how they'd watched each other without breathing for a while, for perhaps ten seconds, before the first of them, a woman the same age as the one they were already forgetting about, fished out the abandoned newspaper from the side of her seat and started reading.

The dying art of small wants

Luton Echo 'Pick Yourself A Bargain' column

5th June

MOUNTAIN FOR SALE
Rarely climbed, some recent erosion. Sky extra.

FOREST WANTED
For collaborative environmental and life project.

STONE GODDESS
Weather marked but still desirable, seeks solid ground.

* * *

12th June

SPACE OFFERED
Still to be cleared but proven capable of containing heavy objects. No strings.

FREE GROVE
To first genuine offer. No timewasters please. Must have own axe.

* * *

19th June

MOUNTAIN STILL AVAILABLE
Owner will throw in sky as goodwill gesture but stars extra.
Buyer must collect.

WASHING LINE WANTED
Must be long enough to reach from oak tree to birch, and
to take the weight of dashed hopes.

* * *

26th June

ATTENTION FOREST SEEKER
Please contact me, have lost your details

EXTRA SUNLIGHT — RENTAL AGREEMENT ONLY
Temporary offer of two hours extra daytime.

* * *

3rd July

STONE PLINTH
Due to relocation, this attractive base could be yours. Some
wobbles, but heavenly vibes included.

TREE FOR HIRE
Some light rope damage but no fallen boughs. Roots not
included.

LAST CHANCE FOR MOUNTAIN
Bear, Orion, Sirius included. Top product already tested
for thoughts. Guarantees and warranties can be shown.
Delivery available.

I come from kitchen tables

across three countries and four English counties. I am from good plain food, bone broth and porridge, farmers digging barehanded in black soil for potatoes, women searching for medicine in hedgerows. I'm from *serve the men first, clean plates or no seconds, think of starving children*. I'm from steamed puddings swimming in custard, sweets only on Fridays. I'm from no talk of sex or church or politics, but I *am* from all three. I am from the status quo, the silent majority, upturned dishes and broken glass.

But writing this now at my kitchen table, I want to invite all those I am from to take a seat. I'll pour the tea, we are from *a good cuppa solves everything*, and *shh*, I'll tell myself, *if you can't say something nice*. So I'll listen not to where I'm from but where we are all going, like when a black and white photograph gets coloured in and we gasp at how it could be now, as if it isn't now, as if the past is something kept in an old shoebox found when a house is cleared, as if it isn't sitting there at our wooden kitchen tables every day.

Safekeeping

You keep the skeleton where you found it, crumpled at the bottom of your aunt's old wardrobe. It's safe there. You whisper to it often, sitting cross-legged on the floor and peering through the keyhole, hoping it'll believe you. At night, you imagine it folding itself through the slight gap between the wardrobe doors, bone by bone, a clattering as it finally lets the last limb out, before marching through the rooms, searching for someone who's like you but not you.

Your aunt was an unusual woman, that's what everyone says. You still laugh at the expression on your cousin's freckled face when you loaded the wardrobe on to the removal van you'd brought with you to the funeral. Perhaps you should have waited for the sherry and nibbles to be finished, but you couldn't bear to see all those pudgy tearful strangers leaning against the wardrobe in case their weight might spring open the doors.

After breakfast, every weekday morning, you put on your suit, pick up your briefcase and leave your house to the skeleton. You do this mostly so that when you come back in the evening, you can pause on the doorstep and listen in case you can catch something – a trace of chatter, of piano music, a kettle boiling, of something, anything, other than yourself.

'Did my mother leave you that wardrobe?' your cousin asks again and again on the phone. 'What makes you think you could just take it like that? She was my mother, not yours. Any secrets she might have had are mine, not yours.'

You aren't sure if you bear or bare a soul. Or even if it's a soul or sole. You or ewe. Your cousin is wrong. It was you who was trusted with your aunt's secrets. But when the phone rings again and you know it's your cousin, you go to the wardrobe, and although you're in a rush because you've only got eight rings before the answerphone kicks in, you still wait until you've smoothed the wood quiet with your hands before you finally unlock it. The skeleton looks as if it hasn't moved since your aunt first lay it there. You run to the door. Sit on the doorstep as you hear your cousin's voice ring out through the house.

The skeleton takes longer than you thought it would. You feel its knuckles first, a heaviness on your shoulder, and then the slight tilt as the world shifts its balance a little and the skeleton sits down next to you. Your cousin is still shouting in the background, still ranting about secrets that are hers not yours, but the skeleton's here, taking your hand now, and you're both safe.

Catching a train with Godot

We missed the first one.

I did think about getting on without him, but there'd be too much confusion later so I stayed where we'd agreed to meet. And after all, fifteen minutes late is early by his standards. I watched as a woman rushed through the barrier at the last minute, her wheeled case careering behind her like an over-excited dog, her eyes raw from crying. Or maybe it was the wind. I'd been standing in the station so long I had no idea what the weather was like outside.

After the train had pulled out, and the woman had stopped shouting at the guard who hadn't let her on, I looked around. There's always a shift in energy when a train leaves. A sigh of relief, or was it regret?

I'd not made a decision on my own for so long that I'd forgotten how to, so I stayed still. Across the concourse, a guy in a black hat sat down at the piano left for the public to show off on. He ran his fingers across the keys at first, back and forth, but then he began to play. I watched the commuters stop and listen. Even the crying woman pulled her case over to a bench and sat still, her face in her hands.

I thought this would be a good time for Godot to come. 'Remember the piano,' I'd say years later. 'God, he was good,' Godot would finish for me, and I'd tease him about all the missed trains, how long he'd made me wait.

The piano player carried on, it was like a concert we'd all bought tickets together for. I tried to store up the notes so I could play them for Godot later, maybe tap them out on his back. We'd laugh at how the station announcements fitted in with the music. A railway symphony, I'd call it.

I fiddled in my pocket as if I was looking for change to tip the orchestra, my nails flicking through the wad of tickets I kept there. You couldn't be too prepared, not if you were travelling with Godot. There's a game I like to play, to let my fingers pick out a ticket for me blindly and it's only when I pull it out of my pocket that I see where we could be travelling to. Haslemere, or Plymouth. Once I even got one to a place called Strawberry Hill.

Godot would have liked it there, if he'd come that day.

'I'm going to get some tea, do you want me to get you a cup?'

I looked up to see the crying woman standing over me, her case obedient now, sitting at her heels.

I shook my head. I didn't meet her eyes, looking instead at a ticket on the ground that someone must have dropped. She was half-standing on it. What if it was the one Godot and I needed?

'I'm waiting for someone,' I told her.

'Aren't we all?' She did this strange laugh then and walked off.

Rattle rattle went her case behind her, as the piano played on.

Waves

Because the doctor said she could do with a change of scenery, he rented a little blue fisherman's house for them in Cornwall. Because it was out of season they got a good deal but because she'd left behind her friends and family and everything she held dear including the streets she'd walked down so briefly with her pram, she cried for days, and because she was crying so loudly that the house became unbearable, he took to walking along the seafront. Because he didn't want to stand out too much – she'd told him once how locals had hounded D H Lawrence and his wife because Frieda wore red stockings – he began to copy the fishermen he saw, walking with his hands looped behind his back, his eyes out to sea. Because it's difficult to walk without looking where you are going, and because it was sometimes misty and the wind so raw that he wore a scarf halfway up his face, he fell in the sea more than once. Luckily, because there were so many fishermen around, he was quickly rescued, but because no one could understand why a grown man couldn't keep out of the water, the rumours began that he was a drunk, or wanted to commit suicide, or perhaps he was just fed up with a crying wife. Because wouldn't you be? Because no one else would now talk to them, and because he couldn't stop looking out to the sea, they began to spend evenings together in their little clifftop garden, her crying and him looking. Because there's only so much time you can bear like this, one night, she turned to him and asked what he was staring at. Because he was a bit of a bore, to be honest, she expected a lecture on the density of stars or how climate change was affecting oceans and ice levels in the Arctic, or even how although grief takes people different ways, maybe it was time for her to listen to everyone and make an effort to move on, and because of this, when he simply said, 'the horizon', she was touched. Because of this, she followed his gaze, thought at first that the haze was her tears but then saw it was fog, and realised that this was how he was seeing the world, and that actually she might be seeing clearer than him, and because neither wanted to talk any more they just spent the night looking out, breaking their silence occasionally by calling out new words for it, 'murk', 'vapour', 'drizzle', and because she had done English Literature at university, while he'd studied Engineering, she carried on longer than him, 'brume,' 'haar' and 'gloaming'. Because she had forgotten the joy of playing, it took her some time to realise she'd stopped crying, and because he was a sore loser, it took him even longer, but because by then they had both got so cold in the garden, they stayed close in bed that night. And because it was a better day the next morning, they made a sudden decision to go back to London. Because he was a creature of habit, he decided to go for one last walk, his hands looped behind his back. Because the horizon was clear, it held little interest for him so he looked around instead, saw the men nodding at him, realised the fishing was actually more of a tourist attraction and because it wasn't holiday season anymore everyone was bored, and that actually, the sight of a man falling in the sea must have been funny. Because of this, he stopped still and shocked himself with something he realised was a laugh. And because it had been so long, for him and for her, the sound of it carried like a seagull all the way to that blue house on the cliff edge, and because, without all the crying, she had done the packing already, she came out to see what was happening. And because the gloaming, the haar, the brume, the murk had gone, she saw him, saw him waving up at her, and because her heart skipped a little bit and she'd thought it was dead, she waved back.

LOSS

the end takes them both by surprise,
happening as it does on an otherwise ordinary day

Home

The first time they visit, the village is as steady as horn-rimmed grandparents glimpsed waving out of the passenger wing mirror of a white Rover. *Just a weekend*, he whispers to Kate. It's as dull as hell, the threat of staying.

Ten years later, barbed wire tears at his shirt, surely they once cruised across this field unimpeded? The spot where he and Kate first kissed is planted with plastic bottles where there used to be beans and spray-painted across the old grocery store he sees, like a stain, the words 'Go home'. Empty houses waiting to be caught by weekenders who will whip them back to shape. Even as a cow paces behind him and a cockerel crows somewhere in the distance, he's still not quite sure if it's the village turning its back on him, or he on it.

Now, the third time, the village doesn't recognise them. It puts on its best face, a face for visitors, for tourists. It's so pretty, the light slow and golden, and they can almost imagine living here, bringing up country children with red cheeks and torn trousers. They avoid the barbed wire, the watching windows, and remember instead their first kiss. The peace of it all. He's not even looking over to where, somewhere behind him, a white Rover drives past, a hand waving from the passenger seat.

The butcher, the tailor's girl
and the witch ball

No one in the house noticed that the witch ball had smashed until a shard of glass entered the soft flesh of the girl's foot. The pain was the same as when the Tailor had instructed her to sleep one night in the Butcher's shop, although then she'd been left with blood on each thigh. Now her foot was unblemished. It was only when she looked up and saw the jagged glass edges that she smiled.

The Tailor took down the ball before any customers spotted the damage. He needn't have bothered because they looked at the girl instead, how she balanced on one foot, head down. Even the ones who'd never noticed her before stared at her doing nothing.

The girl's hands were rarely quiet. At night, she would sew pictures from scraps of red fabric left over from the Tailor's work, showing the clouds and outlines of buildings she could see from behind the counter. That evening she painted the Butcher. Her scissors rounded out his bull neck and stubby hands until the cloth was transformed into a portrait that everyone would recognise. She even twisted a strand of grey and red cotton to form a bloody knife in his hand.

The Tailor's wife clapped to see it but didn't notice how the girl had also cut out a sliver of blue military felt, laid it so it was escaping from the corner of the picture, the sides laced with sharp silver pins. Not too many to be noticed, but enough for her needs.

A week later, the Butcher came to dinner.

He raised his eyebrows as the Tailor's wife served him herself.

The girl is indisposed just now, the Tailor said tetchily. He had been embarrassed that afternoon when a soldier had complained of a tear in his new jacket. Although the Tailor suspected it had something to do with the girl, he couldn't ask her. She'd changed since the witch ball had broken and the truth was both he and his wife were wary of her. This dinner was just one thing they couldn't risk her spoiling.

The evening did not go well. The wine was sour and the custard was curdled. But the gift of a picture the Tailor's girl had made was a nice gesture. The Butcher laughed to see himself like that.

Only as he was leaving did he notice that the new red witch ball above the door did not look as if it was made of glass but was soft to touch instead. It was lumpy in places as if it were a carcass caught in a web.

He shook his head at the fancy, but as he passed under it, he felt a drop like water on his neck. When he put his fingers there, they smelt sticky and metallic like after carving and as he shifted the picture to his other hand he felt a stabbing in his side.

He cursed. He had lost his favourite knife recently, and splinters were so hard to get rid of.

Spinning the kaleidoscope

There were two and then there was one. 'We can only save one,' the mother was told. 'Otherwise both will die.' Luckily she didn't have to choose which baby. Nature did that for her.

* * *

When he's born, Eric has a completely round mind. The mother rejoices how there's no corner for dark clouds to hide in, tries to imagine the endlessly hopeful horizon he looks out on.

* * *

A newborn baby is designed to carry its own weight. Put it over a washing line, for example, and it will instinctively clutch the line, letting itself dangle there. Maybe one day, they'll all get stronger.

* * *

The first dent in Eric's mind comes at midnight just a month after his birth. The father brings him through, 'Didn't you hear him cry?', but the mother is still blurry from medication. It is only when she sees Eric's dagger-glare of accusation that she wakes up. She knows the new crack across his eyes will stay.

* * *

Blur, separate. Blur, separate.

* * *

It sometimes feels like they are a pretend family. 'We have just the one child,' the father will tell people. 'Two,' whispers the mother.

* * *

'Do you think he misses her?' the mother says. 'Do you think he knows he is only half of what he should be?' 'We could try for another,' the father suggests. 'Finish the pattern,' she nods. That night she takes no medication.

* * *

In the morning, she goes to the garden and stands over the washing line. Her hands rest on the rope as Eric runs round and round. He comes to a sudden stop as a wasp buzzes to his right, a butterfly lands on a daisy to his left, and a leaf falls from the sycamore just in front of him, but then he sees her again, holds his arms outstretched.

* * *

Twins hold hands in the womb, a doctor told her once. Now she takes Eric's hands, lets him dance with her, both laughing at their shadows. How beautiful it must be in his mind. A beehive dripping with honey. One endlessly repeating pattern.

Clapping

It started where it shouldn't, but always does, with his lips fastened on home, the sweetness filling him and all he has to do is be a baby.

'You're too old for that.' A sharp slap followed by a spoonful of mashed potato he's not allowed to spit out, the spoon waving towards him like an aeroplane. He's no longer mummy's boy. He's a good boy, a hungry boy.

Other things form in his mouth, called words; sounds beginning to fit together to bring him everything he wants now he's a talker.

Playing in the garden, when, *shh*, a cousin calls him over to a hole in the hedge. Staying silent as he watches the couple moving like music, like a waltz, or was it war? He watches open and dry mouthed as they form words between them that he knows he'll understand too if only he can stay there a little longer. Voyeur, they call out, and it sounds so pretty, so sweet, a peeping tom.

The world's a pantry cupboard left open and he's a scavenger on the spice shelf, putting tastes together just because he can. He's working his way from aniseed to za'atar until one day he unscrews a top without thinking. Stops thinking as he loses sense. Fills with every sense.

The splinters in his heart mean to hold his body a certain way increases the sharpness of the pain, to let his mind wander causes a dull throb. He leaves people behind to concentrate on art, allows the stream of invoices to plug his gaps, and he listens, fingers steepled, as others call him a connoisseur.

External is all. He cheers up the drabness he feels with potted plants, builds bridges around his world so no one is sure whether he is coming or going. He calls everyone darling, although he reserves his fondest strokes for the wine bottle. A drinker? Not him.

She's dabbing his forehead when he wakes up. 'Can I call you nurse?' he jokes. She doesn't smile but says yes, it's her name. He shouts it out across wards, and corridors, and theatres. Rings bells to get her to come running. She's a hole in the hedge, sweetness and words waltzing, she's bottles knocked over and treasures hunted down, she's bunches of grapes and everything he wants. 'Your name, your name?' He wants to taste it in his mouth to see how they fit together. Now she's his darling, he's happy to be patient.

New life

He's standing at the back of the bookshop lift when she gets in. As he does that shifting back thing men always do these days when faced with her stomach, she turns her back on him because it's safer. She's had seven months to see how it's always the ones who give her the most space at the beginning who end up encroaching.

* * *

He is Ben Lewis. She is Mary Carter. Ben is looking to buy a book for his mother's birthday, something cookery or gardeny always goes down well. Mary is looking for the first book she'll read to her baby once it's born.

* * *

She presses the button for the seventh floor, and tries not to breathe as he leans forward to press five. But even this minimal contact is enough to get him talking. 'When is it due?' he asks, smiling when she says another month. 'To think there's new life inside you,' he says. 'I can't imagine what that must feel like.'

* * *

Ben Lewis's mother longs for her first grandchild. She cooks and gardens while she waits, and though his wife says they should tell her that they don't want to have children, he resists because he knows it'll break her heart. Mary Carter has always wanted a big family. Four children at least. She's had an easy pregnancy, and her doctor keeps talking about her childbearing hips as if Mary should agree this is a good thing.

* * *

'Could I?' Ben stutters as the doors open and close on an empty second floor. The shelves of books on foreign languages and music seem to wink at them. 'Please could I touch it?'

* * *

Ben suddenly knows he'll die if he doesn't have a child.

* * *

Mary shuts her eyes as this stranger's hands rest lightly on her stomach. 'A new life,' he repeats. After he leaves the lift, she presses her forehead against the mirror to feel the cold glass against her skin. In the time it has taken the lift to reach level five, Mary has been colonised, consumed, by a life that isn't hers anymore.

* * *

Ben buys his mother a book about roses. Mary leaves the shop without buying anything.

* * *

'There was this woman,' Ben falls to his knees to beg his wife later that evening. 'Oh please darling, please can we think again.' 'No,' Mary will tell her husband, 'nothing happened today.'

* * *

Ben and his wife have four children. Mary and her husband have just one. Her hips may be fine but her nerves, it seems, are not childbearing. Years later, Ben's son and Mary's daughter end up marrying. Although Ben and Mary don't remember ever meeting before, she will watch Ben put his hand on her daughter's stomach and want to punch him. She doesn't know why but, as she's learnt to do, she blames herself. 'New life,' she'll mutter, smiling along with everyone else. It makes everything possible.

Ward back bird black

13. Later than usual, and excited because of the snow, her children rush into the kitchen. Her daughter stands with her face pressed hard against the window, counting every snowflake that lands on the pane as her son drops and catches the ball he's holding with every flake his sister notices. When her husband comes back from work, she kisses him. Tells him that no, nothing interesting happened today. He leans over her, puts one finger into the saucepan to taste as she pretends to slap his hand with the spoon. It's what they always do. The same rhythm as always in the kitchen, the snow muffling all other sounds except, two hundred and sixty-seven, her daughter counts, tick, tock, bounces her son's ball. She's glad she never wrote that note for him. Outside a white moth knocks at the window, shocking them all. Two hundred and sixty-eight, she says.

12. At least the flowers left for him are real, albeit a dusty bouquet that was probably fading even before it was left by the shiny brass memorial plaque with his name on. She takes one petal, her shoulders tensed as if she's waiting for someone to stop her. It's so cold and silent here. She fingers the velvety softness of the white petal, rolls it into a ball like a letter she already knows she'll throw away later.

11. The only place she can think of to go to is the library. It's as quiet as a church, or as silent as she remembers a church to be. It's been a long time since she prayed. She rustles through local newspapers, traces her way back and forth through internet searches. When she eventually finds the death notice, she moans and a man writing in the margins of an Indian cookery book tells her to shush. She asks him for his pen, writes the address on her hand. She's missed the funeral, but at least she can say some kind of goodbye. When she gives the pen back, she sees what he's been writing. Go home. Again and again, next to recipes for mango chutney, lemony dhal, and prawn curries. Go home. But she doesn't take the hint. She needs something to prove that it was real. It's the least she can do.

10. Didn't you know he took his life? Just two weeks ago. Such a shock. But if she had known, would she have needed to ask if anyone knew how he was? No, she shakes her head even as she's sitting in front of her own computer. No. No. No. She doesn't want to be alone with this knowledge, so she runs to the only place she can think of.

9. Time passes so quickly once she steps back into the real world and it's not until several years later, one afternoon on her own, that she thinks of him again. Out of curiosity, she searches for him on the university website but he's not there anymore. Not only that, but the housing department doesn't exist on its own either, it's been swallowed up by architecture – all those sharp corners and black and white photographs he hated. She

forces herself on to Facebook, joins a graduate forum and gets a message she didn't want to read. Despite the peace she's been feeling lately, she really didn't.

8. She threatens him with the police. And he says fine, that he won't bother her again if that's what she really wants, and then that's it, nothing, nada, as she waits, patiently, to be cured by time.

7. He won't let her go without a fight, hanging around out-side her office block until people start to talk. Eventually she's forced to look for a new job. I thought you loved it there, her husband asks, and she kisses him instead of replying. He looks so surprised, so happy. I love you, she says, because love is just a word now. Was that all it ever was? She starts to get silent calls to her home, text messages with just a question mark, and, I am hurting, a handwritten card popped through her letterbox. Why can't he just disappear? What has she ever done to him that he should threaten her so?

6. The end takes them both by surprise, happening as it does on an otherwise ordinary day. They're walking through London with nowhere to go, but the anonym-ous streets are the only place where it's safe to hold hands or to stop in doorways to kiss. But suddenly she looks at him and sees that he isn't anything special. He's just a lecturer in housing. And she's just an admin executive. And they were just two people pretending to be a couple. She knows what it's like to pretend to be someone. She's done it too long. She looks at him, still smiling down at her, and tells him the truth. That she wants a real life.

Her own life. Brutal maybe, too sharp. Apparently you can't do that, just break cleanly, and maybe she already knows that, because she's realised she could never do that to her husband and children, let her family go.

5. She wants only to talk to him, he wants only to talk to her. Even when they're not together, he tells her, he's thinking of everything he wants to say. He wants to know what will happen to all these words that must have been hidden inside him for so long. If you die, he says, I will drill a hole through your coffin and keep whispering to you. She tells him that's creepy, although there's reassurance in knowing she'll never be alone. If you die, she says, how will I know? Who will tell me? She threatens to write a pro forma note for him to carry around with him at all times: if I should die then please return me to... He laughs, tells her that the two of them will never come to an end.

4. It's a new experience for her, this wanting. Every minute without kissing, or thinking about kissing him, is wasted. She'll be brushing her daughter's hair, packing her son's lunch, and will have to stop, look down at her hands and feel weak with wanting him. Even when she's with the people she loves best, should love best, she wants him.

3. They can't look at each other. That's how she knows it's getting serious. They have lunch together on campus most days now, and she's pushing a baked potato of all things round her plate when he suddenly holds out his hand to her and says, let's go. They walk round campus

as he points out birds' nests to her. It's another project he's set his students. They have to map all the homes they can see, he says, but of course they'll miss these. He says it's to make the point that sometimes we need to look beyond our own experiences.

2. She's starting to smile a little more these days. Even her husband says she's happier, that maybe she's coming through… he still can't say the words in case it becomes real, a solid part of their family. Depression. So she says it for him, agreeing she feels better, even though she can't look at him.

1. He passes her a tissue, this stranger who comes to sit next to her on the grass mound outside the university library, where she's been watching students dipping in and out of little dens made out of sticks. He doesn't say anything until after she's mopped her tears, and then he tells her that it's a project his students do every year. He gets them to make shelters out of things they can pick up for free on campus. It's not meant to be upsetting, he says, and for some reason, she confides that it's just the way she is these days, she can't help it. He nods. Mature student? he asks, and she says, no, admin. Never could see the point of university to be honest, which makes working here now a little ironic. He's wearing the kind of wool jumper, tartan scarf, and tweed jacket that shouts out academic. Social housing, he says. Though to be honest I'm not very good at the social bit. Whereas you, he looks at her, hands her another tissue and shakes his head. No, you're not too good at it either. And, so suddenly it takes them both by surprise, they smile.

Things that used to feel safe

If you make a snow angel on your own so no one can see you do it, is it real? And if no one claps when you swish your arms up and down to make wings, will it ever fly? You don't care, you do it anyway because that's what you've always done when it snows. So you lie on the grass outside your parents' home and you make angels. Not just one, not just two, soon there's a full circle of angels. You imagine how they'd glow if only you could look down on them from your old bedroom. Spectacular, you can hear your younger self say. You imagine how your old dog would have barked at you from the kitchen. You almost hear the kettle whistle as your mother makes another cup of tea, the rustle as your father turns over another page of his newspaper and complains to your mother about how you'll be catching your death. You make another angel, and another, filling in the gaps until the circle becomes a whirr of wings. You get up, brush the snow off your clothes, but when you go to sit in your car, you can't open the door because the bonnet is crumpled so hard that bits of the engine are spilling over the seats. The airbags are as white and soft as the snow that's still falling. 'Drive safely,' your mother had told you earlier that evening, as she put on the kettle. 'Why does she need to go out at all in this weather?' your father had complained, turning another page of his newspaper. 'I'll be back before you know it,' was what you'd said, but now you need to be gone before they get back from the hospital. You turn for one last look at the angels. You hope that at least they'll be some comfort to your mother and father. That they'll remember it was what you always used to do every time it snowed.

The new Fairbourne paint chart

*In 26 years – or sooner, if forecasts worsen or
a storm breaches the sea defences – a taskforce led by
Gwynedd council will begin to move the
850 residents of Fairbourne out of their homes.*
– The Guardian, May 2019

SEASIDE RETIREMENT
A restful blue, this lighter version of our more common
MONDAY MORNING, has been named after dog walks,
teatime scones and empty beaches.

COASTAL COMMUNITY
A soft yellow designed to conjure the sound of distant
laughter, cups of tea and cardigans lightly shrugged on
shoulders.

WELSH WEATHER
A combination of slate grey and forest green, will change in
every light and reflect the many shades of rain.

TWENTY-SIX YEARS
A mirage-like pink, inspired by damp corners in living
rooms and the old marks of suitcases wheeled over wet
sand. Some customers claim it is remarkably long lasting.

WAKE UP CALL

A dramatic red designed to rouse and galvanise, best used as a statement wall.

EROSION

A true blue darkening and building for a lasting impact. Goes well with…

DECOMMISSION

A dominant striking grey more commonly found on battleships and factories.

DERELICT HOME

Often used in combination with BUNGALOW and STATIC CARAVAN, this subtle and yet unforgettable beige is proving surprisingly popular.

CLIMATE CHANGE DENIAL

Disclaimer: This colour has been temporarily removed by our legal department.

Not every silence needs to be broken

One Tuesday afternoon in May, she sits at an open door shelling the broad beans she's grown herself, and as each empty shell hits the tin bucket by her feet it seems to sing along with her about how while they are eating tonight, she'll look around the table at her friends and family, and in that moment just before she joins them in laughter, her heart will settle in her body as if it remembers where it belongs. Peace. There have been so many times in her life when the only point of relishing contentment has been knowing that it won't last, but now she puts the beans aside for a moment, looks out at the courtyard where a swallow is swooping in the slight breeze that makes her shut her eyes briefly, and when she opens them again the swallow is still darting here and there so she knows it's moving for pleasure, no other reason, and that makes her happy too. There'll be an empty place at the table tonight, as there has been since last February, and everyone will pretend to ignore it but she's tired of that. The last shells fall into the bucket. She knows she's prepared too many but he did love beans. She lets her fingers brush along the soft down inside the final shell, the curves where the beans had sat, the way the shell had grown round them like this house had once grown round the two of them. Half empty now. Tonight she'll take away his chair, and as she raises her glass to where it would have been, she'll encourage every-one to share their memories, even to sing him back into the room and into their lives again. She tilts her head up to

the sun, just for the pleasure of it. A full bowl on her knee.
A full house. It's more than enough.

George's house has two chimneys

Perhaps it would have been better if one was for everyday and one for Sunday, like how your mother makes you change dresses. She only has one necklace though, and sometimes she'll let you wear it on Sundays.

'I've only got one neck,' she laughs, as if that makes any kind of sense.

George's two chimneys both work every day though, sputtering out smoke which, if you stand in the wrong place, catches at your throat.

On Sundays, you stand in the kitchen, and ask your father to do up your zipper. Although your Sunday dress is getting too small for you, you like to feel it tighten round you as the zip goes up, just as your mother positions dishes in the oven for lunch. They'll be left to simmer while you three walk round the village, walk past George's house.

There are no trees round George's house anymore. He's cut them down for wood to feed his two chimneys. Compared to the other houses in the village, this makes George's house look bare and defenceless. It seems to float on stilts, whereas all the other houses – your house – lie flat to the ground.

The night the storm comes, the wind is the first thing you notice, rustling through what's left of the trees, and then the gale howling like the man you saw once in the forest on your Sunday walk, before your father moved you on. After that, it's the rain pattering, and then knocking, and then striking against your roof. Your father yells at you and your mother to stay still, to move downstairs, to run upstairs.

Your mother lets you wear her necklace as a treat even though it's not a Sunday. Just so long as you stop crying.

Your father says this is George's fault for being so greedy and that we need the trees, otherwise we'll all wash away.

You wonder what that means, to wash away, and if it's something to do with crying. You watch George's house from your window, the large one with squares that you can trace round with your fingertips. You like how your face fits exactly in each one of them. You've tried them all. There's one for every day of the week, and more.

Today, there's no smoke coming from either of the two chimneys on George's house, but they are stretched up so high like they are hands waving, a drowning man asking for help. You clutch at your mother's necklace, and then, putting your face in every pane of the window, you smear the glass with your tears.

HOME

what if we finally start living?

Swoop

He's given her concrete slippers and she couldn't be happier. She tells him they are the colour of the fuchsia flowers she used to twiddle between her fingers. They were ballet dancers before – fell swoop – they crashed down to the ground.

'With one fell swoop,' he corrects. 'It's not an action, it's a thing.'

Fell swoop, she masticates the words under her breath like a grungy adolescent. Fell swoop, she slices through the air like a martial warrior.

Fell swoop, she runs into him like a train wreck.

Her eye's too bad for work the next morning. 'They'll never believe you,' he says. 'No one would believe just how clumsy you are.'

She cooks him lemon meringue pie, crushes enough Valium in the egg whites to tranquilize a bull. He drinks the beer as if there's a drought, before moving on to the merlot she won in the office raffle. 'Mar-lot,' she says, deliberately over-pronouncing the T because he likes to correct her and she needs him in a good mood.

She sips orange juice from a beaker because her lip's still swollen. 'People would pay a fortune for a mouth like that,' he says. 'Trout lips, or something, they call them.'

She holds out the pie but he shakes his head. Do drugs oxidise? What if this takes too long and he tastes them? He's still dwelling on trout lips, searching through his mind for something he knows is there but is hiding from him. 'Trout pout,' he shouts at last, before taking up the bowl, and then he eats, staring at her all the while as if he knows what she's hiding and he's going to search her out.

When he falls, it's not the victory she imagines. She doesn't look at where he's lying, as she slips off her concrete slippers, and bare-footed, twirling as if she's a ballet dancer, she runs fell swoop down the road and far away.

Buried

We only discovered Mum had double-booked her own funeral after she'd died.

I met my brother off the train from Northampton clutching the file marked 'funeral' that I'd found amongst her papers. She'd stipulated which crematorium she wanted, named the poems and prayers to be read, the songs to be sung. She even gave a list of which relatives and friends she wanted to be there.

However, it turned out that my brother had a similar file which she'd sent to him the week before she died. His file contained her request for a woodland burial, with a detailed planting plan of the bulbs and perennials she wanted. Even the list of relatives and friends who should stand up to say how much they love her was different.

We sat in the station bar drinking Guinness and agreed this was typical of our mother. 'She was always looking at how she could be the centre of attention,' my brother said, but then he told me his funeral was best because it was ecologically sustainable. My brother is an electrical engineer. I always refused to let him explain exactly what that was because I liked looking at his hands, imagining jagged lightning streaks of electricity from every finger as he waved them around. Even now as he talked about oaks and alliums, I saw sparks. I was planning to cry if he insisted on the woods, but just then our phones beeped simultaneously. It was our father, fresh off the plane from Spain.

DO NOTHING UNTIL I AM WITH YOU. The same text to both of us. We weren't sure if he had forgotten to take off the caps lock or if, by the magic power he had always possessed, he knew we'd been arguing.

Our father made himself at home in our mother's house. He pulled out a bottle of white wine from the fridge, and told us he was getting married again. Then he said that it was our mother's final wish to combine her funeral and his wedding in one ceremony.

I could tell my brother considered this as doubtful as I did, but at that moment Dad's fiancée walked into the kitchen. Lorraine was wearing one of my mother's dresses, but with a huge belt tied so tightly round the middle that she looked like a cottage loaf. This was emphasised by her skin, baked brown by the sun as if she had spent too long in the oven.

Lorraine, my new stepmother-to-be, was thirty-five, two years younger than me, and one year older than my brother. She told us that she and my father met at a bar, but now my father doesn't take a drop. That's how Lorraine put it, take a drop. I was busy repeating this in my head so I almost missed it when she said we were to call her Mum, and that she would take care of everything for us now.

Something about the way she said that made me wonder if she was my father's nurse, but if so, she wasn't a good one. My father may not be drinking in public but he still had the red face and too sweet smell of an alcoholic. Even now, he alternated making increasingly desperate phone calls to try to find a vicar who would perform the double ceremony with nipping outside every five minutes. My brother and I fell back into our old bad habits too as we made excuses for him to Lorraine, but she just smiled.

'Shall we go girlie wedding shopping together?' she asked me, and when my brother snorted I blushed but I still didn't say no. My mother and I had never gone shopping together in the way my friends had.

The night before the wedding burial, my brother came to get me and we crept into the funeral home. It turned out he had bribed the undertaker to let us dress my mother in white. We took the flowers that were supposed to go on top of the coffin and surrounded my mother with them so none of the red silk lining showed. She looked as if she was lying in a meadow. I brushed out her hair, and my brother put her hands round a wreath so it looked like a bridal bouquet. Then we asked the undertaker to close the coffin.

It gave us some comfort to think of our mother like this the next day. Her coffin lay behind my father and Lorraine while they exchanged vows, so she wouldn't miss out on anything. None of the friends and family my mother wanted for both her funerals came once they heard about the wedding; my brother and I were the only guests. Neither of us had won, but we hadn't lost either.

Although my brother refused to have anything to do with Lorraine afterwards, I liked how she kept in touch. She always signed her cards *Mum* followed by lines of kisses and I counted them every time to make sure she was not losing interest in me. And although her presents were so glittery that even my seven-year-old daughter rejected them, they were like magpie treasure for me. I spent whole evenings painting my nails in different pastel colours, putting butterfly clips in my hair and choosing which scented gel pen – nearly always strawberry – I would use to plan my own funerals.

Go Jack, go

'A paper,' Jack's wife says. 'Go to the shop and come back with it. That's all.'

She puts money in his hand. Pay. Paper. pa-pa-pa-pa.

'Are you listening?' His wife's eyes are shining. He doesn't like to see her cry.

'A newspaper, Jack. Just once. For me, love.'

Love.

She loves him, but not in that way anymore. Because nowadays, when he loves her in that way, he isn't gentle. No, Jack. No.

The door shuts behind him. He's in the street, where he follows two schoolgirls who turn to laugh at him until he gets nearer. Then they start to scream, run.

No. Trouble.

For once don't get into trouble, Jack.

Trow. Blue.

Blue. Blow. Bubbles.

He's swimming in a cauldron of bubbles. Don't get wet. Take your trousers off. She'll be cross if you get your clothes all mucky.

A man now. Manhandling.

'You don't want to do that, mate. Not here, eh?'

All the bubbles pop.

Pop. Po-po-pa.

'Can I help you?' A woman now but no girls. He's sure he'd been following laughing girls.

Just once, Jack.

'Shall I call the police?'

NO!

He runs. No police. Not this time. Just once. Buckle trousers like she's taught.

Police. Polite. Be polite, Jack. People don't realise. They don't know. They're just trying to be kind.

'Hello.'

Hell. Devil. Hot. Please, no police. I can be polite.

Pol-pol-pol.

Ite.

'Don't get too close to him. You don't know what he'll do.'

He'll do nothing. He's just Jack.

'What's that in his hand? Give me that. I promise no one will hurt you.'

Hurt. So much hurting. Her crying, his love. Hand. Holding so tight.

'Open your hand, son.'

Son. Sun. Hot like hell. Oh-pen. Good boy, Jack. He opens. Mouth.

Women screaming. Pan-de-moan-I-mum. Pa-pa-pa-pa.

'Paper,' he says, lifting clenched hands.

So proud. So proud she'll be when he comes home.

'What's he saying?'

'Love, I think.'

'Paper,' he says. 'Jack get paper.'

Click-click-click.

One woman turns to slap a boy. 'Don't you dare put his photo on Facebook,' she says.

Jack laughs.

A book like a face. His face in a book.

She likes books. Does she like his face? Not like that, Jack. Not anymore.

'If you just come with me, sir.'

So polite, police.

Po-po-po.

It's a procession and it's all for him, and there she is. Holding a Facebook to her ear, shouting she can see him now.

'Am I in a book?' he asks, as they get in a car.

A polite car.

Po-po-ca-ca-pa-pa.

'Paper,' he says. 'Get a paper. Just once.'

'Oh Jack,' she says. 'I'm sorry. I thought you could do it.'

He opens his hands to show her the coins he's kept safe for her so he doesn't have to see her cry.

Five woldland walks

1.

Every Sunday afternoon your family goes to the woods. 'But doesn't Mum want to come?' It seems not. Besides she'd spoil the fun by getting nervous as you balance like an underage drunk, a tightrope walker tottering along fallen tree trunks to collect that coin Dad puts out to tempt you on to the end. The higher the drop the tree rests over, the bigger, the better, the coin. Often you fall, but more usually you fear the falling and jump first. Decades later, you wonder if this is the lesson your father wanted you to learn. That all you have to do to win is to keep your nerves steady. Because even if you nearly reach the end, even if you fall and hurt yourself, even if you're pushed off by your brother, he won't relent. He just smiles as he puts the treasure back in his pocket. And you walk on to the next tree. Because there always is another fallen tree. Just as there always was another Sunday.

2.

Seventeen, and the boy you're not yet allowed to call your boyfriend takes you to the woods as it gets dark. You pretend to be spooked by the birds so you can take the hand he gives up to you when no one else can see. He even smiles as you trace the spider's web with your finger on his palm, and then up his arm. His beautiful arm that you have a sudden frightening desire to bite until he starts to tell you a story about a couple whose car broke down in the woods. The boy went to find help and the girl dozed until she heard a banging on the roof. When she opened her eyes, she found herself looking at the upside down eyes of her boyfriend on the other side of the car window. But it was hard to see because the window was smeared with, what? Blood. And then she saw another head looking in at her. But this was attached to a body. And that body was trying to get in the car now. And no one knew she was there. No one was coming to help. You've heard this story before. Who hasn't. But never in the woods. Never at night told by a boy who won't call himself your boyfriend yet. And who knows you are there? No one. You open your mouth to scream but then he kisses you. Takes your fingertips that have only seconds ago been etching out an imaginary trail of blood on the window and sucks them gently. And suddenly you'd open any door just so long as he holds out his hand to you. This boy, who you'll call husband before too long.

3.

You're in Africa on an island that was once the holiday paradise of Zanzibar spice dealers. A paradise where they kept their slaves. And once you know this, it's hard to stop noticing the particular facial characteristics of everyone you meet. That narrowness of a forehead. That hook of a nose. And then once you hear this story, it's hard to stop looking up at the tall trees that fringe the beach. It seems the young wife of a slave owner wanted to know if a monkey would fall from a tree in the same way as a coconut does. And because she asked and asked, he sent a slave up to the top of the tallest tree and then shot him dead, just so the wife would stop asking. But history doesn't record whether the man – I presume the slave was a man – curled up like a ball or fell, arms and legs outstretched, taking up more space than he had ever been allowed alive. History doesn't record whether anyone cared. Whether the wife was ashamed. Whether she stopped asking questions. Whether she was even watching. Because it's such a paradise, this island with all the tall trees that fringe the beach.

4.

A perfect Christmas, and now you're watching your son and daughter run through the woods in front of you, their new woollen hats like bobbing festive baubles amongst the trees. You breathe in and smell the tang of pine, the crack of a twig under your boots, the frosting of cold air on your cheeks, and your fingers brushing over the chocolate coins you've kept hidden in your pocket for a surprise later. And all is good until you see the children stop dead. Your heart flutters – a dead body, an accident – until you see it. One small tree deep in the wood, festooned with coloured ribbons and hand-written wishes. And suddenly it's enough. Your children might not believe in Father Christmas anymore, you'll soon have to bribe them to play cards with Granny, diets will kick in and moods explode, but you – and they – will always have this. Their faces turning to you, that look of wonder, a gift given with no expectation, a light in the woods.

5.

It's a dream you often have. Of walking through a wood and picking sleep straight from a tree. Sleep is green, slightly underripe, and its skin has a bloom that clears like mist from a window as your thumb rubs backwards and forwards over the surface. When you cup it in one hand it gives slightly under the squeeze of your fingers. Sometimes you have to pull a branch down to reach the sweetest, deepest, longest fruit. Sometimes it will be protected by thorns but always, when you put it close to your face, you'll smell your grandmother's room – the musty chemical tang of crocheted cushions, endless cups of tea, pie crust and the special potion she'd make herself to keep her brass ornaments shining. And just as you never questioned why she kept going, you never question why you need sleep to make itself so freely, so abundantly, available. You just keep picking it. As if it will always be there for you.

Homegrown

Sheila is trying out the new garden swing; she's got her white wine spritzer, her ciggie and her 'sex and shopping' saga, but when she tries to sit down the darn thing turns her arse-over-head, sprawled out on the lawn as the sodding thing sways this way and that, sparkling at her in the sunlight.

* * *

Graham is in the greenhouse, pricking out seeds. How many in each packet? He'll lie to Sheila later that it's hard work, and that he doesn't really enjoy dipping his fingers in the soil, waggling them in front of her face so she can see his dirt-encrusted nails. Later in bed, she'll imagine a seed dislodged from under a nail, how it takes root inside her. Sheila will wake up choking from the green tendrils in her throat, opening her mouth to a blossom storm.

* * *

Sheila wants to pick the first tomato. She remembers from childhood how her granddad would hold them close to let her inhale their peppery goodness, her teeth biting through skin. She's been watching the plants closely, seeing them turn from green to orange to red. There's one she thinks is perfect, and as her hand goes out to twist it free, a snail starts to climb up her arm.

Shhh… Graham is taking Sheila to see the bird's nest. He's been following the birds for days. Laughing at how they stumble, even in flight, due to the weight of the sticks in their mouths. He wants to cover Sheila's eyes to make the most of the surprise, but as they get near, he spots the hair that the birds have used in their construction. It can't be Beth's hair, not so long after, but it's red. Like Beth's. He steers Sheila another way, his hand tight against her face now, and says he can't find it. Perhaps the birds decided not to nest there after all.

* * *

Sheila's not sure the meat should be raw inside. Or burnt outside. Why can't they just microwave it all anyway? Why isn't Graham like other men who refuse to let their wives barbecue? Why does he keep going off to the end of the garden where he'd thought the birds were? As if she cared. She's never liked birds. She tips the entire meal in the compost bin. Why can't you remember you can't put meat in the compost, Graham will ask her later. It was organic. That's what she'll say. As if natural made everything better.

* * *

Graham has to watch the chicks learn to fly on his own because he's sworn to Sheila that they haven't nested in the garden. Not this year. He ignores the way she clutches her belly because he doesn't think she realises what she's doing. He holds his breath as each one takes flight, not sure what he's hoping for. A red flag maybe. The trail that will lead him astray again. But each bird is direct and sure, landing safe. He goes to find Sheila. To tell her the news.

Bookmarked

The best – and the worst – thing about working in a second-hand bookshop was finding the things that people left inside old books. Once Jan found a slice of onion that must have been used as a bookmark. In defence of the previous owner, it had been a cookbook, but even so. You wouldn't expect to read a gardening book and get scratched by a cactus, or open a bible and be struck by a miracle.

The second best thing is the customers. Her favourite dresses up to match the book he wants to buy. It's become a game between them. She has to guess the theme before he gets over the shop threshold. Once he was strapped to an ironing board, its folded legs bashing into anyone who walked too near him. 'Housework,' she hazarded. 'The Joy of Cleaning.' But it turned out he wanted to read about chemistry. 'I'm an ion,' he said in his phlegmatic way. 'Have you noticed that no one ever pronounces the R in iron?'

'It really doesn't matter to me,' she replied. But he looked upset then, so she had to explain she was playing too. She'd been anti-matter.

After that he started coming in nearly every day. They're both competitive so to make sure she wins, she has learnt how to use her shop displays as a form of subliminal nudging. She leans railway books against the till, and sure enough he's dressed as a train driver the next day. Sports books are almost too easy, but maps are interesting. The day he dresses as Devon – a full cream tea – becomes a red letter day for them both. She closes the shop so she can enjoy the scones with him.

Today though, he has her puzzled. From his goggles, woolly hat and the skis he's balanced on one shoulder, she can tell he's some sort of skier. But he shakes his head when she gets out the skiing books. And the mountain books. Even the travel guides for Switzerland, Austria, and France get dismissed. She has her back to him, searching the racks for novels about snow when she hears a yell, a crack and the tumble of several shelves of books. When she spins round, he is on his knees.

'Shall I call an ambulance?' she shouts. 'Have you had an accident?' Of course, she's thinking, medical books, first aid, doctors. He's cunning, she'll say that for him.

But it turns out this is his idea of a proposal. He wants them to take off together, to slide into the unknown.

She says yes. There's a possibility of danger, even of a whiteout, but there's also exhilaration, joy and a nice mug of hot chocolate at the end. And if they had been a book, her smile would be the bookmark.

Foresight

Mercury is retrograde again this week, and Violet says I need to be careful with my communication channels. I pay her £60 for an hour every Tuesday so she can tell me things like this to look out for. We sit in what she calls her consulting room while she holds my hand. Sometimes she will keep her eyes shut for the whole of our time together and I'll stare at her bookshelves, trying not to hate the sensation of my fingers in her sweaty palm. She has a surprising number of bad novels, the kind I pick up and throw away on holidays because they're the kind of books you should only read on the beach. But shouldn't psychics be more spiritual? She has her eyes shut so, as she tells me about my week ahead, I watch the dusty crow jumbled up with the other ephemera on top of her shelf. The bird's eyes are bright green, which I'm sure crows' aren't. I remember how she told me it was her first attempt at taxidermy, and I suddenly know this will be my last time with Violet. When she's finished, I'll tell her that I want a better class of reader to tell me what my future holds. My tongue will be like quicksilver, my mind clearly made up. But for now we stay sitting, latched together with my hand caught in a grip as sticky as molasses and we listen as Mercury moves swiftly between us.

Bull in a china shop

She tells me about a dog she met in the Sahara who would carry teabags around in its mouth. It would bite the bag open before licking the spilled leaves up gently. A different flavour every time.

'That must have been bad for its heart,' I say.

She says how once she slept out in the desert and the stars had curved around her and it made her sad how most people saw the sky as a dull straight line.

I say nothing. I'm one of the dull straight ones.

In the same place, this desert, she had heard a story about a man who moved so fast through life that the village wise man tied him to a post, leaving him there until his soul had time to catch up with his body. She herself had walked along dry riverbeds and picked up so many fossils that she'd ended up leaving them there.

It's where they belong, I don't say.

I have never been to a desert or slept out under a night sky. I wrest dangerous food from dogs, and the thought that I might be descended from a fossilised fish makes me feel sick.

I'd chosen her because she looked out of place in the café. She'd been picking up the deliberately mismatched cups and saucers to study the makers' marks as if it was a language she needed to learn. I like quiet people with wide shoulders. The type of person who always ends up with small busy partners, following them meekly through life.

I am not a small busy person but I do know that quiet

people are not always as interesting as they seem. Allowances are made because they are never given the chance to get a word in but too often they just have nothing to say. They fade out of life, these quiet types, whereas their partners get busier and busier. In every relationship, it seems it will always be someone's duty to fill the spaces.

This is why I am still single. As a large quiet woman, the people I like pass me by, but I have not given up hope. I thought she and I might be perfectly matched cups and saucers, and by speaking the same silence we could fill our own space. But then she started talking.

The force of her sentences nudge at me, knock me down, overpower me. She asks me questions only so she can tell me the answers. Did I know, she asks, that Blaise Pascal had a special pocket sewn into his coat for the account of the two hours in which he met God? Before I can ask who Blaise Pascal is, she's telling me of the morning she saw a moonrise at the same time as a sunrise, and who she would most like to motorcycle across Africa with.

She taps her cup against the saucer so it clinks with every sip she takes. Do I know what a quantum computer is? That she has visited an oasis that was ringed with salt? Was I aware that the Berber language is to be spoken not read?

She draws symbols into the mountain of sugar she has poured onto the table between us. The dog was called Lucky, she says, he used to steal the tea bags but one day his luck ran out.

She puts her hand in her pocket and I wonder if she did leave the fossils in the riverbed, or if she has one secreted in her coat. I could never trust someone who has met God, even in the desert. But instead she pulls out a handful of sand and lets it mingle with the spilt sugar.

Then she watches me as I draw a ring with it around the teapot. In our shared silence, we hold our breath, finally catch up with ourselves. It's as if we can taste the stars.

Living room

What if we just change the name to dead room? No, what if we make the room living? What if we paint over everything, the oak furniture, the lights, that expensive sofa we inherited from your mother? And what if you agree it makes you claustrophobic too? What if the dog doesn't get out of the way quick enough? What if we paint him too? Why don't we choose a light green colour, like oak trees just coming into leaf? Why don't we get branches from the park and big fern leaves and stick them to the walls? Why don't we put earth over the carpet? And what if we scoop up ants, caterpillars and worms and bring them in too? What if we keep the windows wide open so birds can fly in? How will we manage when we can't get out of the door because we've painted over it? How will we jump through the windows too? What if we went back and forth bringing in more and more branches from outside? When will we realise that we are building a nest? When will we pull our hair out and shred our clothes to make it soft for us? When will we stop talking and start singing? When will you sing back to me? What if we curl together in our soft nest and let nature look after us? What if we finally start living?

All spoke for

Man-ners

We eat lunch in the dining room on Sundays. Six of us round the table: father, mother, two brothers, two sisters. Sometimes grandparents, uncles, aunts and cousins join us, but never friends because this is family time. As the youngest, it is the best time of the week for me. For once, no one is allowed to have better things to do. Sometimes I even let my fingers float out to touch my sister Annie who sits next to me.

'Mum, Laura's touching me again!'

I withdraw my hands. Let them rest with floppy wrists on the edge of the table. Never elbows, that's bad manners. In front of me, the spoons are facing the forks. The sharp side of knives pointing out, glasses on the right. I even love the ritual of laying the table, so much order to get right.

Your favourite

My Daddy-Granny cooks us a spread every time we visit. Although we, or most of us, tuck in, everyone knows that it's Dad she wants to make happy.

'I've made your favourite,' she'll say, bringing out an egg custard as if by magic.

What she doesn't know, but we do, is that Dad doesn't like egg or custard. He just eats it to please her, and we're not to tell her because to tell the truth will spoil something

143

that isn't anything to do with the dish itself.

When we're staying there, Granddad and I go every Saturday morning to buy Granny a special bar of her favourite chocolate.

'How do you know it's her favourite?' I ask Granddad. I'm this close to spilling the beans about the egg custard, but then he tells me that he loves Granny so much that he knows everything about her.

Later, he will tell everyone he doesn't know what made me cry, and Granny will say something about girls and growing up. When she coos with delight over her chocolate, even though I look very close, I can't tell if she's really pleased or just pretending.

FHB

We have our own family language about food. We all know that when Mum says FHB, we have to wait for visitors to help themselves before we can tuck in. We call pudding afters because for some reason it annoys Mum, and over-pronounce a hard 'a' in strawberries and raspberries to mimic Dad's accent. When dishes are finished, we say they are 'all spoke for, haha' but none of us can remember why.

But each of us eats our food differently. Dad works his way across the plate from left to right; our mother waits until we've all started before beginning her own; my eldest brother George always asks for 'as much as possible of everything' and my second brother William can't eat anything until he has smelt it. As for me, I have always copied my older sister Annie's tastes before even thinking about developing my own.

Annie and I don't like fish, could eat Marmite by the

spoon, can taste custard even when it's hidden in trifle, although soon it seems we don't like pudding at all, and we don't eat potatoes, or crackling, or cake. We'll never have seconds even when we're hungry. Then one day I realise that Annie has stopped eating. Even the tiny bit of roast chicken breast she took has been half pushed under a lettuce leaf.

The rock cake man

Dad is always on a diet. They never last more than a day or two, but one month he keeps to it exceptionally well. The only problem is that he isn't losing weight. Dad, it seems, has a slow metabolism.

Me-ta-bo-lism. I've reached the stage when I would eat words if I could, and this one feels particularly delicious.

Then one day when Mum, Dad and I are in the car driving home, Mum decides she wants to stop at a roadside café for some tea. Dad tries to get her to wait until she's home but she can't understand why he's being so difficult about it.

As we walk in the café, the woman behind the counter shouts out, 'It's the rock cake man!'

It turns out that Dad hasn't been losing weight because he's been eating so many rock cakes that he's been given his own nickname.

'But how did you ever think I wouldn't find out?' Mum keeps asking.

Dad's not clever like Annie. But then it's the fact that she's not eating that Annie's so good at hiding.

Special meal

For our birthdays we are allowed to choose our own meal, and we always pick the same thing every year. George picks sausages and gravy, Will has pancakes, I have stuffed marrow with lashings of cheese sauce, and these days Annie has nothing.

Jack be nimble

Annie takes control of what I eat now. I am allowed biscuits if I choose slimming ones from brands with names such as Harvest Lite and to have the exact number she allocates me. What she doesn't know is that I still raid the normal biscuit tin. In fact, I eat so many that Mum presumes it is both me and Annie tucking in.

But then one evening, Dad eats all three of my diet biscuits in one go as a joke.

'That's Laura's portion,' Annie says.

Dad can't understand why I can't just go and get more.

'She's on a calorie-controlled diet,' Annie explains.

'Laura's a child,' Dad says, staring at me. 'And she's not fat.'

Annie ignores him.

'Jo,' he shouts through to my mother. 'Did you know about this?'

Just a small one

Annie is four years older than me, but although I'm only ten we're the same size. And now I'm growing faster than she is.

Dead man's leg

Apparently we need to act 'normal' around Annie and no one is allowed to mention her weight. When my brother is caught repeating my grandmother's comment, 'so thin', he's sent to his room.

One day Mum asks me what we had for lunch at school and I tell her that all the dishes have special names that make me laugh. We have a currant pudding that's called Spotted Dick, and a jam roll that we call Dead Man's Leg. And I like both smothered in a white custard that's called snow.

I'm telling Mum all this when I stop. Am I being disloyal to Annie who never eats school meals? But Mum's miles away, only noticing when I've stopped talking.

'Carry on,' she says, and so I reel off all the other dishes that we have at school. This time she listens, and it's as if we are both feasting on them. As if we will both never have enough of food being funny, and yummy, and sometimes horrid, but never frightening.

Mummy's chocolate mousse

Twenty years later, Annie and her family come to stay with us. I haven't decided what to cook for our family Sunday lunch, but my children say there can only be one pudding.

They think that my chocolate mousse is famous throughout the world, because my husband once told them so as a joke. My daughter was even caught asking a stranger if he loved 'Mummy's chocolate mousse' too.

'It's our favourite,' they tell their cousins, Annie's daughters. And I ask Annie if she remembers Dad and the egg custard.

We are both laughing so much that soon all our children want to know the story too but none of them can understand it. Why couldn't their granddad just tell his mum that he hated egg custard?

'It's about love,' I say, but I've lost their attention. They're listing their favourite foods instead, much as we used to. We've kept up the tradition of birthday meals, and they've kept up the tradition – without meaning to – of going through lists and lists of different possibilities before opting for the same every year. Shepherd's pie for Sally and toad in the hole for Angus.

Annie and I go into the kitchen and I'm whisking eggs for the chocolate mousse when she tells me, matter-of-factly, that she is finally in therapy for her anorexia.

My hand stops. 'I thought you'd just got a bit thin,' I say.

She looks at me as if I'm stupid. 'Duh,' she says.

'But you weren't in hospital,' I tell her, as if that makes any difference. How did I get to the age I am now without really realising what she had gone through had a proper name?

She shakes her head. 'I could never get anyone in the family to talk about it,' she says. 'It was as if everyone was pretending it wasn't happening.'

No, I want to tell her. We just didn't know what to do, and we all probably thought it was our fault. I know I always blamed myself for taking her place as the youngest in the family. If I could have had just one wish it would have been to have a big sister I could lean on again. Not one I was always afraid of breaking.

Instead I go back to whipping the eggs, carefully melting the chocolate and adding some butter. She shakes her head at the richness of it, and I already know that later she will only take the smallest mouthful, but at least she will take that.

It's a shock to realise that I feel as happy as I used to do at the family Sunday lunch table before Annie stopped eating. Because I'm guessing that when she does take a spoon, she will tell me that it's her favourite now. And when she does that, I will tell her that I'm going to make it for her every time she comes, and it'll be our way of saying how much we really love each other.

FINISH

Self-portrait with chocolate

For two days now, I've been carrying this bar of chocolate in my bag, the red shiny wrapper surprising me when I search for my keys or my purse. Every time, it's an unexpected gift, like finding a fiver in the pocket of last year's winter coat. I sit on the tube imagining opening it, the smell of bedtime drinks in my grandmother's old steamy kitchen rising up to meet the commuters, and already I'm patting the bar through the bag, like this morning I touched my daughter-in-law's stomach to say hello to my grandchild, who we all call Choc Chip. One Christmas, we were given a life size chocolate terrier which sat in our sitting room for months, gently mottling by the radiator, until a guest, uninvited, cut off its head and offered it around. I got half an eye and the nose. *Chocolate is there to be enjoyed*, he said, and he was right. Too often, I've felt guilt, although when we went to St Lucia and saw it growing, we found out how easy it is to crack open each ripe bean and I thought of that dog, that baby who still has to learn to survive in the world, and then this, the bar I want to eat but send to you instead. With love.

Acknowledgements

Thanks are due to these editors for first publishing the following stories:

Waves, *Baltimore Review*; George's house has two chimneys, *The Interpreter's House*; Catching a train with Godot, *Bayou Magazine*; How he likes me to dress, *Everyday Fiction*; Lost librarians and the whale, *Save As Writers*; On Hold, *New Flash Fiction Review*; Safekeeping, *National Flash Fiction Day Anthology*; Instructions for reading this story, *Monkeybicycle*; Ward Back Bird Black, *Brittle Star*; Five Woodland Walks, *Writer in the Garden*; Spinning the Kaleidoscope, *Visual Verse*; Not Sorry, *Cincinnati Review*; Clapping, *Okaydonkey*; Homegrown, *Everyday Fiction*; Tube, *Envoi Magazine*; In the dark no one can hear you scream, *Tears in the Fence*.

Waves was also anthologised in the *Best Small Fictions 2019*, Not Sorry was chosen for the *Best Microfictions 2019*, Lily for the *Best Microfictions 2021* and Clapping was on the *Best British and Irish Flash Fiction 2019-2020* list.

I'm also grateful to the people who have helped bring this book to life.

Firstly my publishers, Valley Press, and in particular Jamie McGarry, my wonderful editor Jo Haywood, Peter Barnfather who came up with the best cover design, and Francesca Eden.

Meg Pokrass continues to offer me, and many other flash writers, constant inspiration as well as the reminder to have fun on the page, and, in no particular order, I would like to thank my writing friends and first readers for their encouragement and friendship, which has been especially valued over the last strange period: Henry Peplow, Vanessa Gebbie, Clare Best, Catherine Smith, Chris Hedley-Dent, Andrea Witzke Slot, Michelle Lovric, Tiffany Murray, Linda Cracknell, Sian Thomas, Jill Munro, and my fellow readers in the Tunbridge Wells RLF Reading Round group.